Stephen
The truck was
towa

Stephen shouted, "Esther! The truck!"
It was all he could get out.

Esther looked up in time to see the truck gaining speed as it rolled toward her. She threw the Frisbee as far as she could. "Ninja, fetch!" Then she dropped and rolled out of the path of the truck.

As Esther desperately moved out of its way, the truck careened down the hill, scattering park-goers, and finally stopped with a loud bang at a large oak tree. Its front fender was dented and the hood now sported a decided buckle to it.

Stephen ran over to where Esther had landed and helped her sit up.

"Are you okay?" he managed to croak out as he brushed leaves and grass off of her.

Esther nodded and leaned on Stephen while she caught her breath.

"That was close!" she gasped.

Books by Tina Ann Middleton

Nikki Dog
Love and Grace

Tina Ann Middleton

Tina Ann Middleton has written poems, essays, and stories since childhood. A voracious reader, she likes to ask, "what if?" and then spin stories from there. Tina describes herself as having an active (and sometimes overactive) imagination.

She and her husband, Darran, have been happily married since 1981 and have two grown daughters. Tina works at a VA Medical Center as administrative support in a Primary Care clinic and greatly enjoys serving Veterans.

She is the author of two independently published books, *Nikki Dog* and *Love and Grace*.

Follow Tina on Facebook and on Twitter -

🅵 https://www.facebook.com/tinaann.middleton

🅩 https://twitter.com/mid_tina

Cover design by Darran Middleton

MISTAKEN TARGET

The Forrestville Series
Book One

Tina Ann Middleton

Shield Of Faith

Publishing

ISBN-13: 978-1-7348336-0-7

Copyright © 2020 by Tina Ann Middleton

Acknowledgments

Writing my first novel has been an adventure. Sometimes I wondered if I was going to make it or if I should just ditch the whole thing and forget about it. But, I didn't, and here it is. This book would NOT have happened without the help of a lot of people and I would like to express my thanks to those who got me started and kept me going in the right direction.

First, I want to thank You, God, for Your awesome love and grace and for the gift of salvation through Your Son, Jesus Christ. I am so grateful to You for giving me the love of reading and the imagination that helped me ask, "What if?" Thank You for helping me follow through and providing people to guide and encourage me on my writing journey.

To my patient and loving husband, Darran, many thanks, hugs, and kisses. You're the one who, after hearing me describe the book I would like to write, sat me down and told me to start writing. You have listened to my ideas for scenes, read my rough drafts endlessly, and encouraged me when I felt that I had no idea what I was doing. (Which I didn't, but that didn't stop us). I feel like this is really more *our* book than *my* book.

Thanks to Kimberly Middleton, our oldest daughter who is also a martial artist. Without your advice my heroine might have done something very foolish and dangerous – twice! Your input helped me keep the story realistic.

Thank you, Jennifer, our youngest daughter, for the time spent discussing my first effort at writing a novel. It means a lot to me that we can share a love for writing.

Thank you, Lenora Worth, for not taking the idea I tried to give to you for a book. Rather, you told me that I should write it. Thank you for your encouraging words along the way.

Thank you, Shannon Mack and other members of our law enforcement community for allowing me to pick your brains about police matters that are part of the story. If there are any errors, they are entirely my own.

Thank you, Robyn Crippen, Virginia Disotell, and Donna Copeland for being my beta readers. Your comments helped me catch errors in the manuscript and provided much-needed encouragement for this budding author.

Thank you, members of NOLA Stars and the local chapter of the American Christian Fiction Writers. The instruction from your workshops and the fellowship I enjoy with other writers is of immense value to me.

Thank you, reader, for picking up my book and reading it. I pray it will entertain and inspire you.

Tina Ann Middleton
May 2020

For God has not given us a spirit of fear, but of power and of love and of a sound mind.

2 Timothy 1:7 (NKJV)

Chapter 1

Early June

"It's a beautiful morning for a run," Esther thought. The light fragrance of flowers mingled with the sharp tang of pine needles tantalized her senses as she paused to admire the clear sky and light, wispy clouds. Esther knew that the heat and humidity would build in by mid-morning. Such was summer in Louisiana. She sighed as she adjusted the scrunchy holding her long brown hair and turned to her jogging partners.

Her brother, Paul, reached down to stretch, his service weapon tucked securely at his back. As a narcotics detective in their small police force, Paul made sure he always had his weapon and his partner, Ninja. The black German Shepherd was Paul's constant shadow.

"Come on guys," Esther urged. "Let's get moving. I want to get done before it gets too hot."

Paul stood up from his stretches and winked at his sister. They set off down the trail, starting slowly, then settled into a jog with Ninja trotting beside Paul.

"Do David and Christy know we're jogging on their trails this morning?" Paul stole a glance at his petite sister.

Esther nodded as she worked to regulate her breathing.

"Yeah, I talked with Christy yesterday. She said she didn't see a problem. She told me to just make sure to close the gate when we're done. They're going with their Sunday School class to a weekend church conference in northeast Oklahoma."

Once she felt she was settled into a steady pace, Esther let her mind wander. She smiled as she glanced at her older brother. It was good to be able to spend time with him again. The two siblings enjoyed a close relationship growing up, but, over time, had allowed distance and busy lives to separate them. After losing both of their parents in an automobile accident, Paul and Esther returned to their childhood closeness. Esther felt that their bond had deepened as they learned to draw on each other's strengths.

Paul saw his sister looking at him and grinned at her. "I'm glad you came with me," he said. "I was afraid you were going to reject me in favor of your history teacher."

Esther blushed and lightly elbowed him in the ribs. "He's not *my* history teacher. He's just someone I met a few weeks ago at the dojo. Don't pester me about him."

"I wouldn't do that – much."

Paul laughed at her, then sobered

"I'm glad you met him. You need to have someone like Stephen in your life, sis."

Esther rolled her eyes at him.

"We're just friends," she countered. "We enjoy some of the same things. That's all."

Paul shook his head. "Esther, you need to let go of that fear. Let yourself experience falling in love. It will be okay."

Esther jogged in silence for a minute.

"I want to, Paul."

She was silent for another minute.

"It's hard."

Paul nodded his understanding, his face softening as he empathized with her emotional struggle.

"I know. But you can't let fear keep you from experiencing God's best for you."

They continued down the trail without talking for a few minutes, then Esther decided to change the subject.

"I saw Kenneth Owens in town yesterday. He didn't smile, but he didn't glare at me like he normally does. He even asked about you."

Paul narrowed his eyes as he turned a sharp look on his sister.

"Esther, I'd rather you stay away from him. After his son died in prison, Owens told me he'd kill me if given half a chance."

"You think he's still bitter that you arrested his son?"

"Well, that's the main issue, especially since Jimmy killed himself in prison. But we were also investigating Ken for drug dealing. We just didn't have enough proof to arrest him when we arrested Jimmy. We know there is someone who is heading up the drug sales in this area; we just haven't been able to nail it down yet.

Esther pondered her brother's words as they moved through the woods. The sudden sharp pain in her leg surprised her so much that she stumbled and almost fell. Paul reached for her elbow.

"You okay?" he asked her, his dark eyes concerned. Esther grimaced as she reached down to rub her leg.

"I've got a doozy of a Charlie horse," she groaned.

"I told you to stretch before we started." Paul reminded her. Esther ignored his brotherly tone as she continued to massage the knotted muscle in her leg.

"You and Ninja go on ahead," she told him. "I'll meet you at the picnic tables."

Paul and Ninja jogged down the trail, soon disappearing from sight on the wooded path. Esther slowly stood and eased her foot down to try to stretch out the cramp. When she could stand on the leg, she limped up and down a short section of trail until she felt confident that she could walk without the cramp returning.

"Gee whiz!" she muttered to herself. "So much for jogging with my brother. By the time I get there he'll be sitting on one of the picnic tables with that smirk on his face."

Esther and Paul had engaged in friendly competition since their teens, always trying to one-up the other in athletics. Because of his job as a narcotics detective, Paul had to stay fit. He ran, swam, and bicycled as well as lifted weights. Esther stayed in shape by running and training in martial arts. They both enjoyed archery and marksmanship. Currently Paul was ahead of Esther in their ongoing competition because of his participation in local races. She knew he had an ultimate goal of participating in the Iron Man Triathlon.

As he emerged from the woods and headed for the path around the pond, Paul was surprised to see two men near the picnic tables that the Michaels had set up in a clearing near the pond. Although he recognized one of them as a well-known businessman in Forrestville, the other man was someone he had seen around town but didn't really know.

Paul felt uneasy seeing the two men here together. What were they doing on the Michaels' property? He saw Ninja's ears stand up and swivel forward. Paul knew the big dog was picking up on something as they approached the men.

"Good morning." The greeting was polite but forced. Paul saw the man's neck muscles bulge in tension. His body language screamed that Paul and Ninja's presence was neither expected nor wanted.

"I'm surprised to see you out so early."

"Yeah, we like to get out while it's still fairly cool." Paul responded. He watched the other man's eyes constantly sweep the area, coming back frequently to glance at Paul and his K9 partner. Ninja stood for a moment, then moved away and started sniffing around. The businessman's eyes widened a fraction as the big dog approached the vehicles parked nearby.

"Well, we don't want to keep you from your exercise." The men started toward their vehicles, a black luxury SUV and a small, older sedan. His sensitive nose quivering, Ninja sat next to the trunk of the sedan. He stared at the back of the vehicle and raised his paw. Paul nodded at his partner.

"Sir, my dog has alerted on your vehicle. I'm going to have to ask you to open your trunk." As he spoke Paul reached for the handgun tucked at his back. Before he could get to his weapon, the businessman already had his gun in his hand. He fired twice, both bullets hitting Paul in the chest.

Ninja snarled and launched his muscular body at the shooter. He clamped his jaws on the man's gun arm and bit down hard. The killer shouted in pain and swore vehemently.

"Get him off of me!"

His companion fired at the dog. Ninja yelped, then collapsed.

Esther had just gotten where she could walk, albeit painfully, if she took it slowly, when gunshots erupted from the direction Paul and Ninja had gone. She lifted up a desperate prayer for her brother and his dog as she limped down the path as fast she could go, her heart hammering.

Esther could hear the sounds of Ninja snarling, a shout of pain, another gunshot, then a yelp.

"Paul!" she tried to scream, but her throat closed in fear. Esther had no thought for her safety. She just wanted to get to her brother.

Esther stumbled out of the woods and saw a small brown sedan and a sleek black SUV speeding up the drive toward the Michaels' front gate. She limped to the edge of the picnic area and saw two forms laying on the ground. Esther cried out and ran to her brother's still body to kneel beside him.

Her hands shaking, she reached to turn her brother over. Blood covered Paul's chest. Esther frantically felt for a pulse, but there was none. His eyes were open, but there was no life in them. Esther cried out, "No! Paul, no! God, please don't take him too!"

As she knelt beside her brother, Esther heard Ninja's soft whine. She watched as her brother's K9 partner crept inch by inch to Paul and licked his face, trying to rouse him. Esther knew the big dog often woke his partner like that in the mornings, but this time Paul did not stir nor awaken. Ninja whined again and laid his head on Paul's chest. Then he closed his eyes and went still. Esther kept vigil beside her brother and his dog, sobbing in hopeless grief and oblivious to everything else around her.

Chapter 2

Six weeks earlier

"Excuse me, I'm looking for Master Todd Williams?"

Stephen directed his question to a petite young woman dressed in a white gi with her hair pulled back in a ponytail. When she looked up to answer him, he was stunned. Wow! She was gorgeous! A fringe of silky brown hair framed a perfectly oval face with soft, creamy skin. Her large brown eyes had green sparkles that drew him in. Belatedly, Stephen realized she was answering his question.

"I'm sorry, I didn't quite catch that,"

"I said class will be starting in a few minutes. You'll be able to meet all of the senseis when we line up. Are you a new student?"

Stephen nodded. "I recently moved back to this area to teach at the Christian school. Someone recommended your dojo. I just hope it's challenging enough. The last one I went to trained men who were mostly black belts. So, I'm used to a pretty intense workout."

He's going down! Esther fumed inwardly at his casual remark as she kept her face placid. He thought he was some kind of hot shot because he trained with *men* who were black belts. She would teach him how challenging the dojo was when she got him on the mat.

Esther tried to fight the zing of attraction that went through her when she looked up into Stephen's face. His face was more rugged than handsome, framed by short brown hair that showed a tendency to curl. She had to struggle to not get lost in his chocolate brown eyes.

She thought about his comment about teaching at the Christian school. Now she knew why he seemed so familiar. When the principal brought the new teacher into her fourth-grade classroom for introductions, Esther had been too busy to stop and chat.

Even with the physical attraction she had experienced when she met him, Esther felt this pompous jerk needed to learn some humility. She would be more than happy to teach it to him.

Class started with the students lined up on one side of the mats and the instructors, the senseis, on the other. The lead sensei began with a few announcements, then introduced their guest.

"Stephen is checking us out tonight to decide if he wants to join our dojo. Let's give him a rousing welcome!"

The class uttered a throaty cheer. Esther joined in the cheer even as she planned how to take him down.

"Esther, would you choose a partner, and demonstrate our first match?"

She smiled and nodded at Stephen.

"How about our new student? We'll give him a chance to see if we're challenging enough for him."

Stephen had the grace to blush but stepped up confidently. He was concerned about sparring with someone as small and delicate as Esther, but figured he could go easy on her and still give a good showing. He knew that while he was checking out the dojo, these skilled martial artists would be checking him out as well.

Wham! Stephen's head spun at the speed and ease with which Esther took him down and made him tap out. He could see she didn't need him to go easy on her at all. Stephen decided he would show her what he could do in the second round.

The two of them bowed to each other, then circled, looking for an opening. Stephen moved first and took Esther down to the mat.

Esther could feel Stephen's well-developed muscles as he worked to get a hold on her. For a moment, she experienced another zing of attraction which was followed by a smothering panic. She hated being on the bottom in this kind of match. It wasn't just a strong sense of competition. Esther felt helpless when she was held down. She allowed the panic to fuel her strength.

Before Stephen could pin her, Esther managed to get on top and hold him. Stephen struggled to gain the upper hand but Esther had him where he could not get free. He tapped the mat in surrender.

As they stood and bowed to each other again, Stephen could see Esther trying to hide a triumphant smile. He seethed at her attitude, but had to admit she was beyond good. That petite frame hid a tigress!

"Well, did we challenge you enough?" Esther asked him sweetly as the class broke up.

Stephen finished tying his shoe and stood.

"Yes, you did. And I would appreciate it if you would not keep throwing my words back at me." He was tired of her attitude. Stephen knew he shouldn't have said that about hoping the dojo would be challenging enough for him. He realized that it smacked of a superiority complex. But she had been throwing it back at him all evening and he was growing increasingly annoyed.

Stephen took a deep breath. Time to calm down, he reminded himself.

"Lord," he prayed, "help me to show a right attitude here."

"How about if the loser buys the winner a cup of coffee?" he offered.

Esther blinked. She wasn't expecting that. She glanced up into his chocolate brown eyes that twinkled back at her. Esther began to feel ashamed of herself. She knew she had verged on very unsportsmanlike behavior during the class.

"Okay," she conceded. "But it's not a date."

When Stephen arched an eyebrow in surprise at her comment, Esther wanted to hide. Why did she say that? He was just being a better sport than she had been all night. He didn't need to know that she was not interested in dating or falling in love.

"Did you say you like to collect old books?" Stephen asked.

"Yes, why?"

Esther took a bite of her chocolate chip cookie and washed it down with a long drink of iced tea. She was enjoying herself immensely. Stephen and she had been talking and laughing for over an hour.

"That's been a passion of mine for years." Stephen pulled out his cell phone and showed her a picture of a wall of books. "That's in my living room," he explained proudly. "Now I'm trying to figure out where to put the rest of my book collection. I keep adding to it."

Esther studied the picture on his phone.

"Where do you get your books? I find mine at estate sales and Goodwill stores."

"Hey, I didn't think about Goodwill. Do you ever go to the big book sale in Shreveport?"

Esther nodded.

"I never miss it. I've found some beauties that way."

She took the last swallow of her tea.

"So, you said you moved back to Forrestville. How long ago did you live here?"

Stephen thought for a minute.

"It's been about ten years. I actually grew up near Forrestville, about five miles out. My parents still live there."

"I don't remember seeing you in school here."

"I was homeschooled," Stephen replied. "With three brothers and two sisters, we just about made our own school."

Esther sat forward, listening with interest.

"Our school actually started as a homeschool co-op," she told him. "After a while, we had so many students that the parents voted to make it a private Christian school. I remember that it took a long time to get all the paperwork and government approvals done. I transferred there in my freshman year of high school. When I finished my teaching degree, the first place I applied was the Christian school."

"Yeah, my mother taught a couple of the co-op classes and my siblings and I came with her. I'm glad I was able to get the history teacher job at Forrestville Christian. The principal asked me to come now since the current teacher won't be able to finish the school year."

Esther nodded.

"I don't know if the principal told you who you're replacing. Her name is Jenny Martin. My church has been praying for her because of the baby coming early. Her class coordinated a big baby shower for her a few weeks ago. They're really going to miss her. She's decided to stay home with the baby. That's how the position came open."

Stephen stopped to pay for their snacks. Esther started to object but Stephen just gave her an impish grin.

"Hey, remember, the loser is buying the winner a cup of coffee, or tea, or something."

Esther laughed.

"Well, okay. This time I'll allow it."

They walked back to their cars in amiable silence. "Do you work at the dojo full time?" Stephen stopped and leaned on his car.

"No, teaching at the dojo is part of my training there. Actually, I teach fourth grade at Forrestville Christian School."

"Now I remember where I've seen you before. Mr. Covington and I came in your classroom but you were in the middle of something and couldn't come talk to us. Do you always welcome new teachers by putting them on the mat?" he teased.

Esther laughed.

"Sure, it keeps them in line."

"So, do you feel you have me in line?"

Stephen moved closer to Esther, crowding her and causing her to have to look up at him. She felt her heart rate and breathing ratchet up. Esther swallowed hard. The smothering panic returned and dissipated the good feelings from the past two hours. Esther's eyes narrowed as she glared at him.

"Back off!"

Stephen moved a step back and stared at Esther. The amiable book lover he had been conversing with was gone. Now his companion was hostile and poised to fight.

Esther shook her head and let out a long breath. "I don't like people in my personal space."

She gave him pointed look and Stephen stepped back again.

"My mistake. I won't do it again."

Esther missed the easy companionship they had shared. She felt responsible for the tension between them now, but he shouldn't have gotten in her space. Esther got in her car and rolled down the window. It just seemed wrong to end the evening like this.

"Thanks for the snack."

Stephen nodded. His eyes were cool and distant.

"You're welcome."

Esther gave him a weak smile.

"Welcome to Forrestville."

Chapter 3

Esther didn't know how long she had been kneeling beside her brother's body when she felt gentle hands lifting her and helping her onto a seat at one of the picnic tables. She looked through tear-blurred eyes into the concerned faces of David and Christy Michaels. At the sight of her friends, she began to sob again.

"Paul's gone! He and Ninja were shot while we were out jogging." She tried to calm down so she could tell them what happened. David and Christy exchanged a serious look.

"Esther, did you see who shot them?" David asked her.

She shook her head. "No, I had to stop to take care of a cramp in my leg. By the time I got here Paul and Ninja were already . . . It all happened so fast!"

Esther tried to take a deep breath, but it was difficult with her crying and shivering.

"I saw two cars driving away, but that's all. Maybe if I hadn't stopped, I could have saved them." Christy sat beside her and pulled her into a comforting hug.

"Sweetie, if you had been with them, you might have been killed too."

David squatted in front of her, his blue eyes intent on Esther.

"Did you see who was driving or their license plates?"

Esther shook her head.

"The cars were too far away. All I could see was that one was a small brown car and the other looked like a black SUV. I couldn't see who was driving."

David looked over at Christy, then back at Esther.

"Do you think they saw you?" he persisted.

Esther shivered again at the thought.

"I . . I don't know," she stammered. "I was just on the edge of the picnic area when I saw the cars. It's still pretty shady there."

Her mind crawled at the idea that her brother's killer could have seen her.

Esther stood watching David and Christy give their statements to the police. She had tried to give hers, but couldn't stop shaking and crying, so the police officer offered to talk to her friends first, then come back to talk to her. A feeling of surrealism swept over her. She kept expecting Paul to come through the trees to ask her what was going on.

She saw Dr. Harris, the veterinarian, arrive and kneel down to examine Ninja. The big dog's injury had bled profusely and he was barely conscious, but they would not know how badly he was hurt until the vet could check him out. She watched the police chief as she and Dr. Harris ran gentle hands over the K9 to check for other injuries.

"Esther?"

She turned to see the young police officer, Sam, standing beside her.

"Do you think you can give me your statement now?"

Esther took a deep breath.

"Yes," she answered, "I think I'm okay now." She wiped the tears from her cheeks and swallowed hard in an attempt to keep further sobs from erupting.

Sam questioned her about what she saw and heard, his face showing deep concern when he heard she had seen the cars. He diligently wrote her description of the vehicles she saw speeding away from the scene. When they finished, Sam took Esther by the elbow and gently walked her to where David and Christy stood waiting.

"The Michaels offered to take you home." When Esther started to object that she could drive herself, he interrupted her, his voice kind but firm.

"Esther, you've been through an immense shock. You are not a safe driver at this time. Please let your friends take you home. We'll contact you if we have any further questions."

After a brief pause, she gave in and walked with David and Christy to their car. She handed David her car keys and turned to slide into the passenger seat next to Christy. When she sat down and buckled in, Esther felt a profound weariness settle over her.

The ride back to her house was quiet. David parked her car in the small carport, then followed the women into the house. Once inside, Christy hurried to the kitchen to fix Esther a cup of tea. Esther plopped down on the couch, then broke down sobbing again, her head cradled in her hands.

"I can't believe this happened!" she cried out. "Why did God let this happen?"

Before David or Christy could reply they heard a knock at the door, then a man's voice.

"What happened? What's going on?"

When they turned to the front door, Stephen stood there with a puzzled look on his face.

"Who are you?"

Christy moved to stand in front of her young friend as she cautiously eyed the stranger.

"It's okay," Esther looked up and made a feeble attempt to wipe her eyes. "He's a friend."

"I'm Stephen Abrams."

Stephen reached to shake David's and Christy's hands. They reluctantly shook, then stepped back to surround Esther.

"I met Esther a few weeks ago at the martial arts school."

Stephen turned his gaze to Esther and noticed the tear tracks on her face. He knelt in front of her and gathered her small cold hands into his, gently chafing them back to warmth.

"What happened, Esther?"

Esther shuddered and held still for a moment, then looked up into Stephen's warm eyes.

"My brother and his K9 partner were shot this morning. I was jogging with him and had to stop for a cramp. While I was stretching, I heard the shots. By the time I got there Paul was dead and Ninja was dying."

Her face contorted in a spasm of grief.

"Why did God take Paul from me? He was all I had. Now he's gone and I have no one!"

She unconsciously began rocking.

"I'm all alone now. I have no one," she whispered.

Stephen reached out to lift her chin.

"Look at me, Esther," he commanded. She raised her tear-drenched eyes to meet his, the sparkle dulled by grief.

"You are not alone," he told her. "You have me. I'll help any way I can."

After a while Christy persuaded Esther to go to her bedroom to lie down.

"You've had a great shock," she told her. "You need to rest."

Esther didn't argue. She just nodded and stumbled to her bedroom.

Although exhausted because of her intense grief, she found herself unable to sleep. Every time she closed her eyes, she saw Paul's dead body on the ground in front of her.

Then she remembered Ninja. She wondered if he would die too or be so badly injured he could no longer serve as a police dog.

As weariness overcame her, Esther decided that if the latter happened, she would ask the police chief to let her keep him. Her eyes closed of their own accord as she quietly hoped she could keep her brother's dog.

While Esther rested, the others sat in her living room, deep in thought. Finally, Stephen broke the silence.

"David, what happened to Esther's brother? How did he die? I know Esther said that he was shot while jogging, but what else happened?"

The older man shook his head, his eyes reflecting the grief of the day and his compassion for Esther.

"I don't really know much more than that. Christy and I were finishing breakfast when we heard gunshots and then Ninja snarling like crazy. We arrived at the picnic area and found Paul dead and Ninja badly injured, but still alive. When we saw Esther collapsed on the ground next to them, we were afraid she had been hurt too. You can't imagine our relief when we found her alive and uninjured."

Stephen swiveled his head to stare at David, his dark eyes intense.

"Did she see the shooters?"

David shook his head. "She said she only arrived as the cars were leaving."

"Do you have any ideas about what happened, why they were shot?" Stephen asked.

David's eyes hardened in anger.

"We think they may have come upon a drug deal. Before the police arrived, I noticed several sets of tire tracks. I also found white powder on the picnic tables that I think might have been cocaine. I showed the powder to the police officer and he took samples. Paul probably came upon them after the drugs were in the trunk of one of the cars. We think Ninja alerted on that trunk, so the drug dealers shot Paul and Ninja."

"Isn't your property fenced? How did drug dealers get in there in the first place?"

Stephen softened his tone. "I'm sorry, I don't mean to sound like I'm interrogating you. I'm just wondering how all this could happen in this small town."

Christy answered before David could reply.

"We've had some trouble lately with trespassers. Our property is fairly large and mostly wooded. Teenagers often like to come out to the woods and ride their four-wheelers on the paths or hang out at the picnic area. We don't use it much unless we have a large gathering."

She paused to take in a shaky breath, her grief welling over in her eyes.

"A lot of people knew we were planning to go with our Sunday School class to a conference in Oklahoma. What they didn't know was that we had to cancel at the last minute because David accepted an important project that needed to be finished ASAP. Whoever did this probably expected us to be gone."

Stephen looked at Esther's bedroom door. Even though he had only known her a short time, he felt strangely protective of Esther. Stephen had hoped to leave the nightmare of drugs and violence behind when he moved to a small town. Now it seemed as if his new friend was right in the middle of it.

Chapter 4

"Esther, I so appreciate your coming over!"

Abigail Matthews reached over and squeezed Esther's hand. In her 60's, Abigail was still a beautiful woman. Her smooth brown skin showed very few wrinkles and her short white hair complemented her appearance. Abigail's eyes could twinkle in fun with the children she loved to work with or soften with care and compassion as they did now.

"I love visiting with you, and of course with Ninja too."

At this Ninja lifted his head and looked at the two women, his sensitive nose quivering at the aroma of chocolate chip cookies. He was too well-trained to actually beg, but if a crumb or two fell on the floor, he would definitely clean it up.

Esther laughed at her dog's expectant expression. "No such luck, big guy," she told him. "I'm not giving up a crumb of these wonderful morsels."

She took another bite of the cookie in her hand and moaned with pleasure.

"Abigail, these chocolate chip cookies are delicious! Can I get the recipe from you?"

"I'd be glad to share my recipe with you. When we finish our snack, we can go back in the kitchen and I'll get it out of my recipe box for you."

The two women sat sipping their coffee in companionable silence for a minute, then Abigail looked tenderly at Esther. "How are you doing, sweet girl? Is it getting any easier? I know grief has its own timetable for each person."

Esther looked down at her plate for a minute, trying to wink back the tears, then back up at her friend.

"It's still very hard sometimes," she admitted. "I miss him so much. I keep thinking I see him in the street, or hear his voice singing in church. Last week I thought I saw him at the gun range. It helps having so many people praying for me and showing their support."

She watched Ninja stand up, turn around, and lay back down with a grunt. She smiled sadly as she watched him settle his nose on the rug and look up at her and Abigail.

"Having Ninja helps because he's good company."

Esther wiped a tear off her cheek and set her plate on the table.

"But it also hurts when I look at him because I realize he would not be my dog if Paul was still alive."

"I'm glad the police chief let you keep him."

"We weren't sure if he was going to make it at first. Even though the bullet didn't hit his heart, it came awfully close. It did do a lot of damage to his shoulder, though. So much that he can't be a police dog any more. I heard that when Police Chief Jones heard that Ninja would live, she whooped so loud people could hear her down the street. I also heard she nearly cried when Dr. Harris told her Ninja could not be a police dog any more. We still stop by the station sometimes so Ninja can visit. They spoil him rotten with treats."

Esther smiled fondly at the big dog.

"I can't help spoiling him myself."

Abigail reached over and patted Esther's hand.

"I completely understand. Ninja is a very special dog. I thought it very appropriate and touching that he was allowed to be a part of Paul's funeral. The whole service was beautiful. It was a wonderful reminder that death has no hold on believers. I couldn't believe all the flowers and mementos that were given. Someone told me the town council sent a huge bouquet of flowers for the funeral."

"Yes, it was lovely. Even Kenneth Owens sent a spray of flowers."

"Isn't he the man that hated your brother because Paul arrested his son for dealing drugs?"

"Yes, it's very sad. The young man was completely spoiled. Going to prison was such a shock to him that he committed suicide. At his son's funeral Mr. Owens vowed to kill Paul. That's why the spray of flowers at Paul's funeral was so unexpected."

They sat in thoughtful silence for a minute. Then Esther lifted her head and smiled.

"A few weeks later Councilman Grayson sent a smaller bouquet. His card said he wanted me to be able to enjoy flowers that were not part of a funeral. I don't really know him very well. He goes to my church, so I see him in passing sometimes. His thoughtful gesture really took me by surprise, especially considering he was out of town at the time. His kindness really touched me."

"Do you think he has romantic ideas about you?"

"Oh, my, no!" Esther shook her head in amusement. "He's old enough to be my father. I think he was just being nice to me because my brother was an officer killed in the line of duty. You know how people are about that. After Paul's funeral I think I received at least a dozen stuffed animals and more dozens of cards from people I don't even know. I think he was just being nice."

Esther finished her cup of coffee and the last bite of her cookie. She wiped her mouth with her napkin, then started picking up the dishes from their snack.

Abigail protested, "Oh no, dear, I'll get those! You're my guest."

Esther laughingly held the cups and saucers away from her friend. "No ma'am, I will get this. You're still recovering from bronchitis, remember?"

Abigail shook her head. "I think I can handle a few dishes. I'm not that sick, you know." Just as the words left her mouth, she started coughing. Esther rubbed her back until the spell ended.

"Right, not that sick," Esther lovingly reproved. "You're not fully recovered yet, you know. If you don't rest and take care of yourself, you won't get well."

Abigail sheepishly conceded and handed her plate and cup to Esther, then got up to walk with her to the kitchen.

"I'll go with you and get that recipe for you. I have a couple more in my box that I think you'll like."

The two women started toward the kitchen. Ninja lifted his head again and started to get up to follow them. Esther thought about his massive body and wagging tail moving around in Abigail's small kitchen and motioned for him to lay down.

"Ninja, stay. I'll be right back."

The shepherd settled back on the rug.

As Esther turned to head to the back of the house where the kitchen was located, she looked out Abigail's large front window and saw a small red hatchback pull up in front of the house. A young man got out of the car and walked up the narrow sidewalk to the house. He was thin and wiry, with long, stringy brown hair and a scraggly beard which did little to hide his acne-scarred face.

Ninja stood up and looked out the window. Without warning, he began barking and snarling viciously. Esther had never seen her dog look like this. With his fur bristling around his face and neck and his gleaming white fangs, he was a terrifying sight.

Esther saw the visitor look at the front window where Ninja was standing and how his eyes widened. As she watched, the young man stood transfixed for a moment and then turned and bolted for his car. He threw the car in gear and peeled out away from the house.

Esther and Abigail stared at each other and then at Ninja in wonder. The big dog's aggressive behavior surprised them.

"Who was that?" Esther asked.

"That was Jesse's friend, Frank Parker." Abigail looked out the window. "I think he was here to pick up Jesse. Our truck is in the shop so Jesse asked Frank to come get him."

"Do you know if Frank has ever used drugs?" Esther stroked Ninja's head thoughtfully. "Maybe Ninja has seen him at a drug bust."

Abigail shook her head.

"I don't know," she admitted. "I haven't really had a chance to get to know the young man. He normally doesn't come in when he comes to pick up Jesse. He just knocks on the door and then waits outside. I've told Jesse to ask him in so I can meet him, but so far that hasn't happened."

Esther stared thoughtfully out the window at the empty street. "That's really strange. I wonder what made Ninja act that way?" she murmured. Esther turned her gaze away from the window.

Ninja was still standing although the fur around his neck lay down and his snarling had turned to an occasional growl from deep in his throat.

Just then Abigail's nephew, Jesse, hurried down the stairs. An attractive young man in his early twenties, his eyes darkened in concern as he came in the room.

"Aunt Abigail, what was Ninja making all that noise about?"

He stopped to put his wallet in his back pocket, then looked up.

"Is Frank here yet? We're going to be late if he doesn't hurry up."

"Oh, Jesse, Ninja scared Frank away." Esther apologized. "For some reason my dog didn't like your friend and I don't think Frank liked Ninja very much right then. Since my dog frightened off your ride, let me take you to work. It's not far out of my way."

"Well, if you're sure it's not too much trouble."

Esther shook her head. "No, it's no trouble. I'm glad to do it."

Jesse gratefully accepted and went to get his lunch from the kitchen.

Esther took the cups and saucers to the kitchen, then returned and took both of Abigail's hands.

"Thank you for the lovely time."

She gently hugged the older woman.

"But you didn't get the recipes," Abigail objected. "Can you wait a minute while I go get them?"

"I really need to get going," Esther apologized. "I have to stop for some groceries and do some work at home. I'll see you at church Sunday and get it from you before the service starts."

"I'll make a copy and bring it with me. Please come back as often as you can." Abigail replied as she returned the hug. "You know you are always welcome."

She reached down to pet Ninja.

"Next time I'll have cookies for you too, fella. Okay?"

Ninja licked her hand. The two women laughed and Esther left with Jesse. Abigail waved goodbye as they pulled away.

"I wonder what made Ninja bark like that at Frank," she mused.

As Esther drove, she chatted with Jesse.

"How do you like your job with the town?"

Jesse was quiet for a minute, then he answered slowly, "It's okay, I guess."

Esther glanced at him with concern.

"Is there something wrong?"

Jesse looked like he wanted to say something, but shook his head.

"No, it's fine. I'm just getting used to things, is all."

Esther wanted to help, but she could see he didn't want to talk about it anymore, so she respected his privacy. They drove the rest of the way without further conversation.

"You can let me out here," he told her when they reached the sidewalk in front of the town hall. "Thanks for the ride. Bye Ninja!"

Jesse quickly got out of the car and headed for the parking lot. Esther saw a thin young man standing by a small red car and heard Jesse call out to him, "Frank! Why didn't you pick me up? I had to get a ride with someone else. I'll sure be glad when my truck is fixed."

Frank looked over where Esther was watching them and quickly turned away. She couldn't hear any more of the conversation between the two young men over the sound of Ninja growling deep in his chest.

Esther stroked the dog's head for moment.

"I don't much like the looks of him either, Ninja," she agreed. "There's just something about him that doesn't seem right."

Ninja lay down in the back seat, growls still rumbling from him. Esther looked at her dog thoughtfully and then in the direction the two young men had taken. She saw them meet up with Richard Grayson and Kenneth Owens. The four men stood in deep conversation for a few minutes, sometimes gesturing toward the manicured lawn of the town hall.

Esther couldn't help contrasting the two businessmen. Ken Owens wore a faded black t-shirt and baggy jeans. His work boots looked dirty and scuffed. His thinning gray hair was cut short but still looked disheveled over his sunburned face.

Richard Grayson, on the other hand, was perfectly groomed. His thick white hair was neatly combed and styled. He wore a lightweight suit of dark blue with a white dress shirt and red tie. His dress shoes were buffed to a high shine.

Esther shook her head as she noticed the glaring difference between the two. It was hard to believe that both of them were wealthy and influential businessmen.

Just then Grayson looked over and saw her. He smiled and waved. Embarrassed to be caught watching them, Esther waved back and drove away.

Esther huffed in exasperation. Her store buggy was trying to go everywhere but where she wanted it to go. She gave it a hard shove and watched in horror as it ran right into another buggy pushed by none other than Kenneth Owens, the last person she wanted to encounter.

She felt a crimson wave of mortification wash over her face. Of all the people in this world for her buggy to crash into!

Kenneth Owens had several interests in town and around the state. The man was one of the few very wealthy in Forrestville. His only son had been badly spoiled and thought he could do anything he wanted. The boy experienced a rude shock when he was arrested by Paul Daniels for dealing drugs and found his daddy's money couldn't get him out of that mess.

After his son's suicide, Ken Owens became rude and surly. He glared at Paul and Esther whenever he saw them. Since Paul's death, Esther had tried to avoid Mr. Owens. Now she had just crashed into his buggy, and, from the look of things, had broken his eggs.

"Oh, Mr. Owens! I am so sorry! Please, let me reimburse you for those eggs."

Kenneth Owens stared at Esther for a long moment, making her feel acutely uncomfortable.

"Where is that mutt that used to be your brother's dog?" he finally demanded. "Didn't he die too?"

"No. He survived."

Esther wondered why he was asking about Ninja. She hoped he didn't see the big dog waiting for her in the car. She also hoped Ninja did not see him. Esther was not sure how her dog would react if he encountered Mr. Owens. After seeing Ninja's reaction to Frank, she was afraid it would not end well.

"The gunshot to his shoulder injured him too severely to be able to continue working with law enforcement, so he's my dog now."

"I see. Well, I suppose you had a hard time of it, hearing about your brother's death."

Esther felt the tears gathering in her eyes and forced them back. She did *not* want to cry in front of this man.

"I was there that day," she informed him, even as she wondered why she was sharing this with him.

"I was in the woods walking out a leg cramp when Paul and Ninja were shot. By the time I got there the killers were gone and Paul was dead. All I saw was two vehicles speeding up the driveway. I barely saw those."

Owens stared at Esther again, his face thoughtful. Then, without a word, he pushed on past her. Esther stood by her buggy, watching him as he exited the store and began loading his groceries into a black SUV.

Chapter 5

Esther hummed as she puttered around her kitchen, cleaning and putting things away. She loved her small, old-fashioned house. The thought occurred to her that the only thing this house needed was someone to share it. Suddenly Stephen's face came to mind. What would it be like to share her home with him as his wife?

She shook her head to dispel the thought. Good grief, Esther thought. I've only known the man a few months and I'm thinking about sharing a house with him. I must be overtired or something. I'm not interested in falling in love.

Esther finished cleaning the kitchen and went to sit in her living room. She had already graded papers for her fourth-grade class and completed lesson plans for the week. Enjoying the chance to just relax, Esther picked up the novel she had been reading and propped her feet up on a small stool. Ninja raised his shaggy head to look at her from his bed and she smiled at him. He was good company on a quiet evening like this.

The novel was engrossing and soon Esther was deep into the plot. The phone rang just as she got to the most exciting part of the story. Esther reached over and picked up her cell phone to check the number. Although it was a local number, it was not one she recognized. She considered letting it go to voicemail, then sighed. Esther knew if she didn't answer it, she'd be wondering who called and wouldn't be able to concentrate on her book until she found out.

"Hello?"

"Good evening, Esther! I hope I'm not disturbing you." Richard Grayson's voice was warm and gracious.

"No, you're not disturbing me at all, Mr. Grayson. How are you this evening?"

Esther lay down her book, curious why the businessman was calling her.

"I'm fine," he answered. "I just felt bad that I didn't get to talk to you for very long after last week's council meeting. I wanted to see how you are holding up after losing your brother this summer. Hearing about his death must have been so hard for you."

Esther paused to swallow her tears. She was tired of crying every time someone mentioned Paul's death.

"I appreciate your concern and your call. I'm doing okay. I was actually there that day. Paul and I went jogging together. I had to stop to work out a leg cramp and by the time I was able to walk again, they had been shot. I found their bodies."

"Oh, my dear! How dreadful for you! To lose your brother and his magnificent dog and to be the one to find them. How horrible that must have been! And how dangerous for you! Did you see who killed them? Are you in any danger now?" Grayson's sympathy was appreciated, but somehow it seemed overdone.

"It was hard losing Paul. You know we were very close. But Ninja survived. He can't be a police dog anymore, so he lives with me. I thought everybody in town knew about this by now."

There was silence for a minute after Esther's last comment. Just when she wondered if he had hung up, she heard him again.

"I'm so sorry I wasn't here for you then, Esther. I had to go out of the country for a few months right around that time. I just got back a week or so ago."

That explained why he didn't know about Ninja, Esther thought, although she wondered why he felt he had to be there for her. They were really more casual acquaintances than friends.

She had known he was out of town at the time of Paul's death. She heard him talking again and turned her attention back to the phone.

"Well, I just wanted to let you know I'm thinking about you. Please let me know if there is anything I can do for you."

"Thank you, it was very nice of you to call."

Esther pushed the button to end the call and tried to go back to her book. The phone call had disrupted her concentration, and now she could not pick up the thread of the story. Esther sighed and tossed the book onto the end table.

"Well, Ninja, I guess I'll go figure out what I want for dinner. Maybe I can read some more later."

Ninja stood and stretched, yawning. He started to trot toward the kitchen, but then changed direction and began sniffing around the front door, his large tail thumping loudly against the wood.

Esther heard a muffled thump and what sounded like a foot kicking at the door. Curious, she peeked out the window in the door and saw Stephen with a bag held in his teeth, two pizza boxes in one hand, and a plastic bag overflowing with junk food in the other.

Esther opened her front door and just stood for a minute watching him juggle before rescuing the pizzas from his unsteady grip.

"Is this a new career for you?" she asked him, laughing. "And which are you, a juggler or a pizza deliveryman?"

"I am stuffed! I don't think I could eat another bite if you forced me."

As he spoke, Stephen couldn't resist checking the pizza box for another slice.

"Stephen, if you eat any more, you're going to explode!"

Esther laughed as she swooped up the nearly empty pizza box before he could grab another piece.

"I'll put this in a baggie for you to take home. There's just enough here for you to have it for lunch tomorrow."

"Getting kind of bossy there, aren't you?"

Stephen glanced quickly at Esther, then grinned.

"However, you are right. Thank you for saving me from myself."

"Thank you for bringing dinner. I was just about to go stare at my refrigerator to see if I could decide what to have. At least Ninja is easy to feed. He just gets dog food."

The K9 perked up his ears when he heard his name. Stephen reached over and rubbed the big dog's head and ears. Ninja turned over for a belly rub which Stephen gladly obliged.

"You're going to spoil my dog," Esther shook her head, smiling. "He already thinks the world revolves around him."

Stephen chuckled. "Well, doesn't it?"

While Esther finished putting away the snacks and throwing away their plates and cups, Stephen stood up to stretch, then wandered around her small living room, stopping at the fireplace to admire the items on the mantel.

There were several decorative cup and saucer sets arranged artistically across the mantel's surface and a few small silk floral arrangements that complemented the sets. Centered on the mantel was a large framed collage with pictures of Paul, Esther, and Ninja as well as pictures of an older couple standing with Paul and Esther. In the middle was a picture of Paul shaking hands with the mayor and holding a medal while Ninja sat between them. Below the picture was an article from the local newspaper detailing a story of how Paul earned the medal. Secured next to Paul's picture was the medal itself.

"It's hard to believe that was a year ago," Esther commented sadly, coming up to stand beside Stephen. She reached out and ran her fingers lightly down the front of the collage.

"How did he earn the medal?" Stephen asked. "It's kind of hard for me to read the article from this angle."

Esther stared at the picture of her brother for so long that Stephen thought she wasn't going to answer. Then she turned to face him.

"It's an interesting story," she replied. "Come sit down and I'll tell it to you."

Stephen sat on the sofa and leaned forward as Esther settled in her recliner. As she got comfortable, Ninja came over and laid his head on the arm of the chair. She stroked his soft fur, the movement soothing her as the memories came.

"Paul told me the whole story. He and Ninja were at City Hall that day. A group of fifth- and sixth-graders was coming for a tour of City Hall and the police station. With a little coaxing from me, Paul had volunteered to lead the tour."

Paul Daniels wondered what his sister had gotten him into as he and Ninja stood watching the children file into the courtroom. They had already toured City Hall and were now settling into their seats to see what an actual trial looked like. Paul smiled when he saw their wide eyes. He knew most people thought of trials the way they were shown on television – with lots of drama and excitement. He looked down at Ninja and chuckled. Ninja looked back, panting slightly, giving the German Shepherd the appearance of laughing.

Suddenly, Ninja stiffened as he craned his head around and his sensitive nose quivered. Paul wondered what had grabbed his dog's attention. His gaze zeroed in on a figure leaving the judge's bench. At first glance, the man appeared to be a city custodial worker. Then Paul noticed the furtive way the man ducked as he walked, keeping his face averted from the gathering crowd. Paul followed his partner, who was now growling deep in his massive chest as he trotted toward the raised dais. Ninja began sniffing around the bench, going behind it to the judge's seat. Then he sat and raised a paw. The dog had alerted on the scent of drugs on a large dirty backpack. Paul looked up to see the bogus custodial worker running down the hall. He started to give chase when he heard Ninja utter a soft whine. The dog was staring intently into the bag and seemed agitated.

Curious about his partner's odd behavior, Paul stepped back and bent over to look more closely at the backpack. A cold chill washed over him when he saw the small electronic device attached to a brick of plastic explosive. The timer showed five minutes left, and it was ticking away. Nausea swirled through Paul's stomach as his gaze swept around the children and other innocent civilians who were gathered in the courtroom for what was supposed to be an ordinary, mundane trial. He knew he had to get the crowd evacuated and the bomb disarmed, but time was against him as the numbers on the clock ticked down.

Praying desperately, Paul looked up and caught the bailiff's eye. The large man hastened over in answer to Paul's silent summons. When the court officer saw the explosive, the color drained from his face. For a moment Paul wondered if the man would faint, but the bailiff pulled himself together and began the difficult job of clearing the room without causing panic.

Already people were curious. The children were standing and pointing where they had seen Ninja sniffing. The guard pasted a smile on his face and explained that the dog had found a dead skunk and they would need to clear the room so that Animal Control could come dispose of it.

At the suggestion of a skunk, people's noses began to wrinkle. One lady whispered to her companion that she thought she had smelled something when she came in. Her friend nodded vigorously, agreeing that an unpleasant odor had been hanging in the air. The children chattered excitedly as they exited the courtroom. Some of the boys tried to hang back to get a glimpse of the dead animal.

Paul could barely keep from groaning in frustration. The crowd was moving much too slowly and he was running out of time. With a quiet prayer for guidance, Paul bent over the device, trying to remember everything he had learned about bombs.

As he examined the explosive, Paul could hear his Academy instructor's voice explaining how to defuse these devices. Willing his hands to not shake, Paul slowly and methodically set about disarming the bomb. When the display went dark, he held his breath, wondering if it would be his last one. Exhaling in relief, Paul slowly removed the hardware from the explosive. He stood and swept the room with his eyes.

Relieved to see the room clear, he called Ninja to him and exited the courthouse.

When Paul and Ninja stepped outside, they were greeted with enthusiastic applause. Surprised, he looked around and found the police chief and the mayor standing nearby. The bailiff had stepped over to the police chief's office to inform her what was happening. One of the teachers had heard him and spread the news.

Police Chief Maggie Jones caught Paul's eyes with a question in her own – was the building safe to enter? At his nod, she and several police officers rushed in to take possession of the explosive and the backpack.

With tears running down his cheeks, the mayor grabbed Paul's hand to shake it, pumping vigorously.

"Thank you," he whispered. "My grandchild is in that group of children. If you had not, if the bomb . . ."

The mayor stopped to swipe his hand across his eyes. He rubbed the top of Ninja's head. "Thank you, too, Ninja."

"Was Ninja trained with explosives too? I thought he was a narcotics dog."

Stephen was puzzled.

"Ninja was trained as a drug dog," Esther explained. "The perpetrator who left the bomb was a drug dealer that the judge had sentenced several years ago. The man had just gotten out of prison and was bent on revenge. He also went right back to the drug trade as soon as he was released. The backpack was one he used to carry his drugs in. That's what Ninja smelled first. He saw the bomb while he was catching the scent of drugs."

"Was he ever caught?"

Esther nodded.

"He was caught hiding in a nearby alley. He wanted to see the courtroom explode. Last I heard, he was in jail in Shreveport, awaiting trial for multiple counts of attempted murder."

She glanced back at Paul's picture and the medal. Esther could almost hear Paul's voice as he tried to tell her that he had just done his job and he didn't see why the town felt the need to make a big fuss over him. She felt a sense of comfort come over her. Sharing the story had made her feel close to him again.

Esther smiled at Stephen.

"Paul told me later that he was 'scared witless' while he was defusing that bomb, but he was praying the whole time. He said he knew God was with him no matter what happened. That's what made him such a good cop. Even when he was going into dangerous situations, he trusted in God and did what had to be done."

Her eyes took on a far-away gaze.

"One of the last things Paul told me was to not let my fear keep me from experiencing God's best for me."

Esther stood and walked back to the mantel. Gazing at her brother's picture, she murmured, "That's a lot easier said than done."

Stephen walked up behind her and gently laid his hands on her shoulders. They stood silently for a moment, then Esther shook her head as if to dispel the somber mood and turned to face him, breaking the physical contact.

"So, did you just feel the need to feed me or was there a purpose to this visit?"

Stephen's face lit up.

"I almost forgot what I wanted to tell you."

He reached into his back pocket and pulled out a folded and wrinkled flyer.

"I found out about a big estate sale just a few miles from here that's going to be held this Saturday. The ad said there are a lot of old books. I thought we could check it out. After we load up on books, we can have a picnic at Forrestville Park."

Esther considered for minute, then, looking at Ninja, slowly shook her head.

"I don't like to leave Ninja for that long right now," she said. "He's getting better, but he's not really ready for me to leave him for several hours."

"What do you do with him when you're at work?"

"He goes with me."

Esther smiled at Stephen's look of surprise.

"Ninja has his own bed next to my desk. He's actually a great incentive for the kids. They earn points with good behavior in class. Those points can be used for the privilege of taking care of Ninja, such as walking him, getting his water or snack, or brushing him. Mr. Covington said my class is always the best-behaved in the school because all of the students want to earn the right to take care of Ninja."

Stephen nodded thoughtfully.

"I could see that," he said. "Gee, maybe I need to get a dog for my class. What do you think, boy?"

Ninja sneezed and the two of them laughed. The big dog cocked his head to look quizzically at them.

"There's your answer."

Esther looked at Stephen apologetically.

"I'm sorry about Saturday. It sounds like it would be a lot of fun."

"Bring him with us."

"What?"

"Bring Ninja with us. He knows how to behave in public, right? I see no problem with him riding along. We can take water and treats for him. We can even take a ball or something for him to fetch. He'll have a great time."

Esther considered his suggestion for a moment, then grinned.

"That sounds great! Hey Ninja, you want to go to a book sale and picnic this Saturday?"

Ninja perked up his ears and barked.

"I think that means yes."

Stephen picked up his keys from the coffee table.

"I'll pick you up at seven. Is that good or will that be too early?"

"Seven is fine. I want to get there early to get the best bargains."

Chapter 6

Esther browsed the stacks of books and magazines. She was delighted at the finds she already had in her arms. The classics she had found were slightly worn, but still in good shape. I'll never run out of books to read, she thought as she glanced a few feet to her left and noticed that Stephen had a good-sized stack of books in his arms as well.

Stephen turned to ask her something just as she moved up to look at another stack of magazines. Startled, Esther backpedaled and nearly fell. Stephen hastily reached out a hand to steady her. When Esther looked up, Stephen's face was just inches from her own. She could feel his warm hand as he supported her while she regained her balance.

For a moment neither moved. They gazed into each other's eyes. Esther felt an unexplained and irresistible urge to throw her arms around Stephen's neck. She looked at his mouth and wondered how it would feel to have his lips on hers. Their eyes met again and the distance between them closed.

A cute little girl of four suddenly darted down the aisle, ducking between their legs, then scampering away from her frazzled mother who was trying to keep a hold on the active preschooler.

"Excuse me, I mean her, I mean us," she muttered as she threw a hasty glance at Stephen and Esther. The woman charged around the corner and swooped up the little girl, who giggled and squirmed.

Stephen looked back at Esther and smiled at her, but the connection was broken. Esther was studying the magazines. He knew she had felt the spark between them, but was trying to avoid his eyes now. Stephen hardly knew what he felt or wanted. He enjoyed the comradeship he and Esther shared. He feared if he tried to exchange it for a romantic relationship, he could lose Esther. Yet, he could not deny the attraction he felt for her.

"Ready to go?"

Esther still wouldn't meet his eyes. She kept her hands busy as she pretended she was occupied with her pile of books and magazines.

"Esther?" Stephen tried to catch her eyes. "Don't hide from me, okay?"

She looked up into his face, and for a moment it seemed she would open up. Then her eyes shuttered and she averted her face.

"Stephen, you knew when we started hanging out together that I am not interested in a romantic relationship. We can be friends, but that's all."

A wave of frustration went through him. He knew he would like to follow up on that spark to see where it would go. The idea of grabbing Esther and planting a kiss on her lips passed through his mind. He wondered what her reaction would be. Stephen stifled a grin. The way Esther was about being grabbed, she would probably put him on the ground.

With a sigh Stephen reached to take the stack of reading materials from her arms. When she pulled away and started to protest, he told her, "Hey, friends help friends, right? I'm helping you not drop these books."

Esther finally met his eyes and searched them for a moment. When she was satisfied that he understood, she grinned back at him.

"Right! And as a friend, I'll even let you carry them to the car."

Esther was relieved that Stephen was not trying to push her into romance. Incredibly, though, she was also disappointed. Disturbed by her mixed-up feelings, Esther hurried to the car. She had to get these wild thoughts of a romantic relationship with Stephen out of her head.

"Go get it, boy!"

Stephen cheered for Ninja as he threw the Frisbee. He watched in disbelief as the dog waited for the disc to land, then picked it up and brought it to him.

"What!" Stephen turned to Esther. "He didn't even try to catch it!"

Esther laughed at his expression.

"Ninja's no dummy," she explained. "He knows jumping for the Frisbee and catching it in his mouth might hurt. That's why he waits for it to land first."

Stephen rubbed Ninja's head.

"Sorry, boy. I forgot about your bad shoulder."

He dug in his pocket and offered the shepherd a doggy treat. Ninja took it gently from Stephen's hand and stepped back to eat it. Then he gazed expectantly at Stephen, his tail wagging.

"What does he want?"

"He wants you to throw the Frisbee again so he can get another treat."

Now Stephen laughed. "Oops! I started something didn't I?"

Esther held out her hand for the colorful disc. "Here, let me throw it."

While Esther and Ninja played with the Frisbee, Stephen looked around. It was a pleasant Fall day, so there were several people relaxing and playing at the park near downtown Forrestville.

Forrestville Park's smooth green lawn was generously dotted with a variety of trees. A playground consisting of three swing sets, a merry-go-round, and a slide rang with laughter as children played. The park sat at the end of the long sloping main street of the town. Several cars were parked at the top of the hill, one of them a classic Ford pickup truck with a sparkling red exterior and cream interior.

Stephen recalled Esther telling him about the owner of the truck. Mr. Winchell was in his eighties and still insisted on driving the old Ford. He was very proud of his classic truck and loved to show it off. While he excelled at preserving its pristine exterior, the elderly man was not good about maintaining its running parts – or its brakes.

The truck had been sitting at the last level place before the street sloped all day while people came and went at the park. Stephen and Esther had noticed several people stopping to admire the classic vehicle.

While Stephen alternated between watching Esther play with Ninja and just looking around, movement at the top of the hill caught his attention. Stephen's eyes widened in shock. The truck was rolling down the hill, straight toward Esther and Ninja!

Stephen shouted, "Esther! The truck!"

It was all he could get out.

Esther looked up in time to see the truck gaining speed as it rolled toward her. She threw the Frisbee as far as she could. "Ninja, fetch!" Then she dropped and rolled out of the path of the truck.

As Esther desperately moved out of its way, the truck careened down the hill, scattering park-goers, and finally stopped with a loud bang at a large oak tree. Its front fender was dented and the hood now sported a decided buckle to it.

Stephen ran over to where Esther had landed and helped her sit up.

"Are you okay?" he managed to croak out as he brushed leaves and grass off of her.

Esther nodded and leaned on Stephen while she caught her breath.

"That was close!" she gasped.

Mr. Winchell came running down into the park, followed by two police officers and several other bystanders. The old man leaned against a tree and gulped for air. He looked mournfully at his prize, then turned his sad eyes to Esther.

"Oh, my dear!" he managed to puff as he tried to catch his breath, his face flushed from the exertion. "Are you all right?"

"If she is, it's no thanks to you!"

One of the officers glared at the old man as he whipped out a black, leather-bound book.

"We've warned you over and over to keep that truck maintained. Now look! The brakes finally failed and Ms. Daniels almost got killed because of it! You're lucky no one was hurt."

Mr. Winchell protested in vain that he had been maintaining the truck and that this incident was not his fault.

The officers did not believe him, however, and issued several citations to the old man.

Stephen and Esther gathered up their things and prepared to leave. The park had lost its charm for them. Ninja came bounding up with the Frisbee in his mouth. He laid it down and looked up at Stephen, who reached in his pocket for another treat.

"That was smart throwing the Frisbee so Ninja would be out of the way of the truck."

Something about that truck rolling right at that time bothered Stephen. He glanced back up at the top of the hill and wondered, what made the truck roll? Was it just bad brakes, or something else?

Chapter 7

Esther took in a deep breath and let it out slowly, enjoying the cool night air as she and Stephen strolled down the sidewalk from the school.

"I think the Parents' Night went well, don't you?"

"Well," he smiled down at her, "you have to remember this is my first year to attend, so I'm still not sure what to expect. But, yeah, I think it was good. You have a good rapport with your students' parents, don't you?"

"I grew up with their younger siblings. It's kind of hard to realize that the kids who were the "mean big sister" or "the snotty big brother" are now moms and dads to the children that I teach."

Stephen stopped her for minute and pointed at the sky.

"Look at all those stars! I'm glad you talked me into walking from your house to the school."

"Yeah, it's a nice walk, isn't it? The weather forecast is for wet and chilly starting tomorrow. I wanted to enjoy this nice weather while I can."

She took a deep breath.

"I love this time of year. The change to cooler weather, the autumn color of the leaves, all of it!"

As they continued on their way, Stephen realized he was falling for Esther in a big way. He admired her gentleness and her quirky sense of humor, her way of bonding with the children she taught, and her ability to enjoy the simplest things – like a walk in the cool, clear October night. He thought about her deepening bond with her brother's former K9 partner.

"How do you think Ninja is doing at the Michaels?"

Esther nudged him with her elbow.

"I know you want to give me a hard time about leaving my dog with a babysitter," she said, laughing.

"Since the shooting Ninja doesn't handle large crowds very well. He's improving, but the crowds still make him nervous. Hopefully he'll be better by the end of this month so he can go with me when we have our Fall Festival. Anyway, he loves hanging out with David and Christy, so I took him over there instead of leaving him alone at the house. They said they'd bring him home for me later this evening."

Stephen shook his head.

"No, I wouldn't give you a hard time about anything you do for him. He's a special dog. I totally respect and honor him as much as I would respect and honor a human cop that was injured in the line of duty."

Esther gave him a sideways hug. "Thank you."

When Stephen returned the hug, she stepped back and looked away. The embrace reminded her that she was becoming increasingly attracted to this strong and gentle man. It seemed she was forgetting much too often that she wanted to maintain a platonic relationship with him.

Esther forced a laugh.

"Don't tell Ninja that you think of him as not human."

As they continued down the sidewalk in an awkward silence, Stephen missed the warmth and camaraderie they had just been sharing.

He opened his mouth to say something, and felt a prickle at the back of his neck. He saw a shadow detach itself from the bushes just ahead of where they were walking and move in their direction.

"Esther," he said under his breath. "Something doesn't look right."

Esther's eyes narrowed as she watched the figure approach them, dressed completely in black, wearing a black ski mask. She felt her defensive instincts rising. The figure was too close for them to evade him. Esther mentally prepared herself to fight.

"Give me your money and your jewelry."

All Esther and Stephen could see of the robber's face was his glittering eyes. He held a gun in his gloved hand. His voice sounded rough and gravelly. Stephen and Esther exchanged an uneasy look.

"Hey!"

The thug called Esther an ugly name.

"Look at *me* when I'm talking to you, not your boyfriend here. I said, give me your money and your jewelry! I'll shoot you if you don't."

To make his point, he waved the gun in front of their eyes.

Then he made his mistake. He reached out to grab Esther's arm. She reached up and grabbed the arm holding the gun, turning the weapon toward his face. The assailant jerked away from her, stumbling back a few steps and dropping the pistol. Then he reached under his jacket and pulled out a knife.

Stephen and Esther separated and moved to either side of the thug, watching him intently. When Stephen stepped forward to disarm him, the assailant jumped to the side in an attempt to evade Stephen.

While Stephen distracted the would-be robber, Esther watched for her chance. As soon as the man turned, Esther's foot shot out and connected with his wrist. The knife flew out of his hands and into the shrubbery nearby.

The thug swore vehemently and charged toward Esther. She moved forward and grabbed his wrist, turning him around and forcing his arm upward at an angle behind his back. Her opponent cursed and struggled, but she held him fast.

Stephen scooped up the gun and emptied the bullets into his hand. His expression was unreadable as he stalked toward the thug. He reached to pull off the mask; but, before he could get to it, the air was split with an unearthly shriek.

Esther was so startled that her grip eased on the assailant's arm. He wrenched away from her and ran off into the dark night, disappearing into the shadows.

Stephen started to give chase, but Esther stopped him. "Don't bother," she said. "We'd never catch him now."

"And let him do this again?" Stephen growled.

He looked as if he was ready to take off. He strained his eyes, looking for the man who had just attacked them.

"We'll call the police," Esther replied. "You have his gun and bullets. Maybe they can trace him that way."

Stephen shook his head.

"He was wearing gloves. Anyway, I think this gun was stolen."

"Why do you think that?"

"I don't know. Call it a hunch."

Esther looked with concern at her friend. Stephen was wound tight. His face was pale and his eyes glittered in a way she had not seen in him before.

"Stephen, what's wrong?" she asked gently.

"What's wrong?!"

He glared at her.

"We just got held at gunpoint! That's what's wrong. You could have been killed, just like . . ."

Stephen choked off his words.

"Just like . . . who?" Esther probed.

"Nothing, never mind."

"Stephen,"

"I said I don't want to talk about it." Stephen bit out the words. "Just drop it, alright?"

"Okay, fine."

Esther was not fine with it, but she sensed that Stephen could not be pushed at this point.

Stephen pulled out his cell phone and placed the call to the police. He and Esther waited in tense silence until a squad car pulled up. Esther watched with narrowed eyes as Stephen stomped over to the police officer to report the incident.

There was something more here.

After giving their statements, Stephen and Esther gladly accepted the offer of a ride the rest of the way to Esther's house.

When they pulled into her driveway, the police officer got out and checked the house and yard.

"Would you like some coffee?" Esther offered.

The officer shook his head.

"No thanks, ma'am. I need to get back to the station."

He shook their hands and got back into his cruiser.

As the police car eased away, Esther closed the door and turned to Stephen.

"How about you?"

She looked closely into his face.

"I think I better offer you some chamomile tea. You're wound tight!"

Stephen gave her a reluctant smile.

"I'm okay," he reassured her. "Just kind of shook up. I'll stay here with you until the Michaels bring Ninja back, okay?"

He sat on the edge of the sofa and tried to look relaxed. Esther watched him for a moment, then settled in her recliner.

"Let's not tell the Michaels about the hold up tonight, okay?"

Stephen looked up from his own thoughts.

"Any particular reason you don't want to tell them?"

"It's late and I don't want to have to tell the whole story again." Esther replied with a weary sigh as she leaned her head back.

Stephen nodded. "Makes sense. We can tell them later. I think they'll want to know."

The sound of a motor brought Esther out of her chair and to the door. She greeted David as he opened the door for Christy. Ninja carefully jumped from the seat to the ground, then trotted over for an enthusiastic hug from Esther.

"How did he do?"

"Just fine," Christy laughed. "I told you he wouldn't be any trouble. We always enjoy having Ninja around. Makes me want a dog of my own."

The Michaels declined Esther's offer of coffee, stating that they needed to get home as they had a busy schedule for the next day. They hugged Esther and shook Stephen's hand.

"Why don't you two join us for dinner this Saturday?" Christy offered. "You can bring Ninja too."

"Yeah," David chimed in. "We can grill some burgers."

Esther looked at Stephen, then nodded their acceptance.

"Sounds good. What do you want me to bring?"

Christy shook her head.

"Just yourselves," she told them. "We'll take care of dinner."

Stephen yawned as they watched the Michaels' sedan drive away. Esther and Ninja followed him back into the house where he grabbed his jacket and keys.

"I'm about ready to go home and get to bed myself," he admitted. "Do you need anything before I go?"

Esther shook her head. She wanted to ask him about his reaction after the hold-up, but this was not the time.

"Lock up after me, okay?"

Stephen reached down and lifted her chin.

"I'm sorry about the way I acted tonight. Give me a little time and I'll be able to talk about it. But for now, please promise me you'll lock up? I won't be able to rest if I don't hear that lock before I leave."

"Well, I don't want to be the cause of you losing sleep," she teased.

Stephen walked out the door and listened as she closed it and slid the bolt in place.

"Too late, you already are," he muttered to himself as he walked to his car.

Esther wandered through her house, a rapidly cooling mug of chamomile tea in her hand. She was too tired to stay up, but too restless to sleep. She finally forced herself to get in her bed and willed herself to relax and go to sleep.

At first, her dream was pleasant. She was jogging in the woods, the same trail she and Paul had jogged dozens of times. Esther was aware of someone jogging beside and slightly behind her. As she moved down the path, she began to feel a growing dread. It settled on her like a deep heaviness that made her stumble with fatigue. She began to realize that the origin of the dread was her companion, but she didn't know why. She tried to look back at the figure jogging beside her, but could not see who it was.

Esther moved out of the woods into the picnic area. She saw her parents and her brother standing in front of the tables, smiling and waving at her. She was so happy to see them that her pace increased. She wanted to hurry to be with them. They opened their arms to welcome her, but then their faces changed from welcome to concern and then fear.

She turned to look behind her and saw a figure dressed completely in black, wearing a black hoodie. As she watched, the figure morphed into Death, complete with his lethal scythe. Esther watched in horror as Death focused on her parents and brother. He swung his scythe and they disappeared. She cried out as she reached for them in vain.

She became aware that Stephen was standing where her family had been. She saw Death turn his deadly gaze on Stephen and ready his scythe again. Esther tried to run to stop what she knew was about to happen but her feet would not move. She screamed, "No!"

Esther shot up in bed, her heart pounding, her breath coming in ragged gasps. Ninja lifted his head. As she sat on the side of the bed trying to calm her racing heart, she felt his cold wet nose nudge her hand.

She stroked Ninja's soft fur. "Thanks, buddy," she murmured. "You were just what I needed."

Esther laid down again, thinking about the nightmare, and wondering about its significance.

"It's just a dream," she told herself.

Chapter 8

"I love all the Fall decorations in town!"

Esther gazed in delight as she and Stephen strolled down Forrestville's main avenue. Stephen walked on the street side with Esther on the inside, near the stores and other businesses. Ninja trotted contentedly next to Esther. Occasionally he would lift his nose and sniff the air. Esther wondered if he was smelling the delicious aromas from the restaurants or if a part of him was still checking for the scent of drugs.

As they approached the corner, Esther glanced up and saw the sign on Carla's Gifts. The insert from her morning paper had advertised an early holiday special.

"Stephen, let's go in here. They've got some good sales on and I want to buy a few early Christmas presents."

"Are you sure that's a good idea?"

Stephen looked in the window at the busy cashier, then down at Ninja.

Esther was puzzled.

"Why wouldn't it be a good idea?"

Then she remembered the last time Ninja was around the clerk working the cash register. Sara was highly allergic to dogs and had suffered a severe asthma attack when Ninja entered the store. Esther had felt bad about the time

Sara spent in the emergency room and had even offered to pay for her visit. Sara just smiled sweetly and declined.

"Oh yeah, you're right. I forgot about Sara's allergies. Last time she got around Ninja, she wound up in the ER. I think it took two shots and a bag full of medicine to clear her up."

Esther hesitated, then asked, "Would you mind staying out here with him while I go in?" She rushed on, "I know what I want. I just need to find them and pay for them."

Stephen joked, "Yes, please pay for them first."

She elbowed him and they both laughed. Stephen motioned to the doors.

"Go ahead, I don't mind at all spending some one-on-one time with my favorite dog."

"Thanks, Stephen." Esther dashed in the door, as if afraid he would change his mind.

Stephen looked down at Ninja.

"Sorry big guy, but we don't want to send Sara to the hospital again."

Ninja just gazed up at him, looking as if he was laughing. Stephen chuckled at the sight.

Suddenly, Ninja's head snapped around to stare across the street. A low, menacing growl rumbled up from his chest. Stephen craned his head, trying to see what had alerted the former K9.

At first, all he could see were townspeople strolling through town and window-shopping; then he glimpsed an acne-scarred face with a straggly beard. Frank Parker glanced furtively in their direction and then in the gift shop windows, where Esther could be seen chatting with the cashier while she paid for her purchases.

Ninja's growls increased in volume as he bared his teeth in a vicious snarl. Stephen tightened his grip on the leash with one hand while his other hand came to rest on the big dog's neck.

"Easy, boy. Take it easy," he spoke to the dog in a low, soothing voice. The last thing he wanted to do today was explain to Esther why her dog had taken off down the street after some punk.

Stephen checked across the street again for Frank, but couldn't see him. Somehow, he had disappeared while Stephen was tending to Ninja. Just thinking about it gave Stephen a feeling of uneasiness. Was he following them? Stephen watched Esther as she picked up her bags and exited the gift shop. Was Frank following Esther?

"What's wrong?"

Esther saw the grim look on Stephen's face and the ruff still standing on Ninja.

Stephen explained about Ninja's reaction to someone he saw across the street.

"I saw Frank Parker sneaking around and watching you through the store windows."

Esther nodded and told Stephen about Ninja's reaction to seeing Frank at Abigail's. Stephen listened with growing concern.

"Esther, there is something not right here. Maybe we need to go see Maggie about this."

"About what, Stephen?"

Esther was exasperated.

"Frank has the right to go wherever he wants in town. As far as we know he hasn't broken any laws."

"What about Ninja's reaction to him? There has to be a reason for that!"

"Oh, right," Esther rolled her eyes. "Maggie, arrest this man because my dog doesn't like him. He ought to get ten to twenty years for that."

Stephen's concern began to change into irritation. Esther was not taking this seriously. As far as he could see, she was entirely too cavalier about her safety.

"Come on," he finally growled. "Let's go home."

"Excuse me?" Esther glared at him. "I don't like your tone. If you don't want to window shop with me anymore, fine! You can go on home. I'm not done."

With that she called Ninja to heel and marched off down the street.

Stephen caught up to her and grabbed her elbow to slow her down so he could talk to her. Esther whipped around and latched onto his wrist. The two stood face-to-face, glaring at each other.

"Don't ever grab me like that again, Stephen!"

Esther's voice was cold and hard.

"I do not like to be grabbed and I *will* take down anyone who tries it."

Stephen stepped back and rubbed the bridge of his nose.

"I apologize for grabbing you," he said stonily. "It won't happen again."

He captured her gaze.

"But I will not stand by and let you endanger your life because you refuse to see that you could be a target. Have you forgotten that your brother's killer is still out there and could have you in his sights?"

Esther froze. Her large, expressive eyes filled with angry tears. "No," she bit out. "I haven't forgotten that at all. But I can take care of myself. I don't need a guardian! So just leave me alone!"

Stephen winced when he saw the tears and heard the sob in her voice. He had not meant to remind her of Paul's death so coldly. He just wanted her to remember she could still be a target and that she needed to be more careful.

Esther abruptly turned and walked down Main Street toward her neighborhood. After she had gone a block, Stephen quietly followed until he saw her enter her front door. He walked back to his car, lost in thought. Esther was fiercely independent and resistant to anyone getting closer than casual friend.

How could he protect her when she didn't want his help?

Esther walked blindly back to her home, fighting tears. She thought Stephen understood her need for independence. She had always had to deal with people who thought she was helpless because of her small size. That was one reason she had decided to practice martial arts.

Her parents and Paul had encouraged her to learn how to protect herself. Learning self-defense had given Esther confidence that she did not need anyone to look out for her. She could take care of herself.

By the time she got home, however, Esther just felt tired. She and Stephen had done a lot of walking before their argument and the hike home had been long. She looked down at Ninja and felt a pang of guilt when she saw the big dog limping.

"I'm sorry, Ninja."

She opened her front door and let the dog in first.

"I didn't think about your bad shoulder."

Ninja limped over to his bed and lay down with a sigh. Esther again felt tears crowd the back of her eyes. She blinked them away and went to put her purchases in the bedroom. When she came back into the living room, she eased down to the floor beside her canine friend.

Esther carefully massaged the injured shoulder.

"I'm sorry, big guy. You shouldn't have to pay the price for my anger at Stephen."

Esther sat on the floor resting and stroking on Ninja. When it started to get dark in the living room, she got up and went into the kitchen to fix a cup of tea for herself and to get Ninja's dinner.

Ninja started to head for his food bowl, then changed direction and went to the front door. When he began sniffing the door and wagging his tail, Esther opened the door.

"Stephen, what are you doing here?"

Esther's voice was cool. She wasn't really angry anymore, but she wasn't ready to talk to him just yet.

"I wanted to make sure you were okay and to give you a peace offering."

Esther stiffened.

"I told you I don't need a guardian."

Stephen just stood there, waiting patiently. Esther shook her head and sighed.

"Come on in."

She stepped back so he could come in, then closed the door.

"What kind of peace offering?"

She was curious when she noticed the paper bag in his hand.

"Turtle fudge."

Stephen handed the bag to Esther and watched to see if she would forgive him.

"I'm sorry I stepped on your independence. I know you are an amazing, strong woman who is quite capable of taking care of herself."

Esther watched his face to see if he would qualify his statement. When he didn't, she nodded and accepted the fragrant peace offering.

"Thank you."

She opened the bag and inhaled the rich, sweet aroma of the fudge.

"Apology accepted."

Stephen stood as if waiting for more. Esther glanced up at him as she took a bite.

"What? Did you want some?"

She started to hand him a piece, but Stephen shook his head.

"No, it's all for you."

He took a deep breath.

"I just need to say, as your friend, I still want to be there to back you up."

Esther regarded him for a long minute, then nodded.

"I can accept that," she conceded. "It's good to have someone to have my back when needed."

As Stephen let out a quiet breath of relief Esther added, "But, I still don't need a guardian."

"How about a comrade in arms, then?" he offered.

"Yeah, I like that."

She gave him a warm smile.

Stephen knew he was forgiven but realized that he would have to tread carefully. He still intended to keep a close watch on Esther; he would just have to make sure she didn't catch him doing it.

Chapter 9

"Miss Daniels, how did Ninja get his name?"

It was late in the afternoon and the children were getting restless and distracted. Robert, a slender and studious boy, had finished his worksheet and was reading a book about martial arts. He held the book open on his desk while he stared at Ninja.

The class all turned their attention to Esther as she finished writing their assignment on the board. She dusted her hands off and sat at her desk. It was almost time to go home, so she thought she had just enough time to answer the question.

"It's kind of a funny story," she replied. "Write down your assignment and I'll tell you."

The children hurried to write their assignment in their notebooks. Esther nodded her approval and began her story.

"He had that name when my brother got him as his partner, but the trainer told us the story the day Paul got Ninja. I came to the station that day to meet my brother's new partner."

Esther wheeled into the Police station parking lot.

"I hope I'm not late," she muttered as she checked her hair in the visor mirror.

She walked quickly toward the kennels in the back of the lot. The new dog would replace Chief, a Belgian Malinois who had reached the age of retirement and would be spending the rest of his days as a beloved family pet with one of the police officers.

"Esther!"

Paul waved to his sister and motioned for her to join him. He was standing next to a tall, well-built man with dark skin and short, gray hair.

That must be the trainer, Esther thought. The man smiled widely at her as if he had a joke he couldn't wait to tell. Paul said something to the man and they both laughed.

"This is my sister, Esther," Paul began the introductions. "Esther, this is Michael Evans. He's the trainer that brought me my new partner."

"It's nice to meet you, Michael. Paul and I have been looking forward to meeting his new K9 partner."

Esther looked down to where a magnificent black German Shepherd was sitting, waiting patiently for orders. He had a thick, glossy coat and a beautiful, plumy tail that he thumped a few times when he saw the three of them looking at him.

"Lady and gentleman, please allow me to present to you one of my best students, Ninja."

It was quite obvious that Michael was very proud of his student.

"He's beautiful, Michael!" Esther exclaimed.

She could see the shepherd's inquisitive brown eyes watching her and Paul as if wondering who they were and what he was supposed to do with them.

Michael beamed.

"He is incredibly smart too," he boasted. "I will show you when we get in the training area."

Paul reached out and let Ninja smell his hand. Then he rubbed the shepherd's neck and back gently. Ninja lifted his head to allow Paul to rub underneath.

"How did he get that name?" Paul inquired. "Is it because of his coloring?"

Michael laughed. "No, it is because he moves so quietly and can seem to appear out of nowhere, like a true ninja."

"That's intriguing." Paul studied his new partner. "Tell me more about this stealthy new partner of mine."

"When he was a puppy, he and his littermates got out of their pen. My family and I searched the neighborhood and found all but one puppy – the little black one. I walked all around my neighborhood and was getting quite concerned that he might have gotten hurt or killed. I stopped on the sidewalk to decide what to do next. I have to tell you, even though I was worried about him, I was also quite exasperated. We had just gotten to the point where we were going to name them and begin training. He was costing me a lot of time. Suddenly I felt a cold nose nudge the back of my leg. I looked down – and there he was! Later a neighbor told me she had seen the puppy following me all the way down the block. I never heard or saw him until he nudged me."

"So, you named him Ninja then?" Esther was amused with the story.

"No, my children did. I picked up the puppy and took him home. When I told the children about what the puppy had done, they shrieked with laughter at the idea of their dad being fooled by this sneaky little puppy. They decided right then that he was a true ninja. That is how he got his name.

Esther's class sat enthralled by the story. Ninja lay on his rug, his ears swiveling toward Esther whenever she mentioned his name. The fourth-grader closest to Ninja turned and gave him a big smile. Ninja thumped his tail and sniffed at the child's proffered hand, finally giving him a lick on the fingers.

"Did Ninja study ninjitsu?"

Robert gazed at the big dog in admiration.

"Maybe he studied when all the others were asleep," another fourth-grader piped up.

"Who knows?" Esther laughed. "Maybe he did."

Stephen chuckled when Esther shared the story with him at dinner.

"I can see why the kids were so fascinated," he said. "That's a great story. I could just see Ninja doing that as a puppy."

Esther grinned at Stephen.

"There's more," she told him. "Would you like to hear the extra good stuff?"

"You bet." Stephen settled back on the couch to hear her story. "I can't wait to hear this."

"I think you'll get a kick out of it," she told him. "It tells about something that has come in handy quite a few times."

Paul opened his front door before Esther could even knock. "Hey, sis!" He gave her a bear hug and ushered her into the living room. "I'm glad you could make it."

Esther knelt on the rug in front of the fireplace to stroke Ninja's back. "How could I stay away? You told me you had something really cool to show me."

Paul grinned and shook his head. "That will come later. Let's go in the kitchen and let me show you the changes I've made. We can also finish getting dinner ready. I'm starved."

He stopped and bent over to whisper something in Ninja's ear, then stood up and moved toward the kitchen, motioning his sister to go ahead of him.

"You're always starved," she retorted. "I think you have <u>two</u> hollow legs. It's not fair you can eat what you want and not get fat."

"I'm just a growing boy," he protested. "I need lots of nourishment. Besides, I work out. That burns off those nasty old calories."

The siblings continued to tease each other as they entered the cozy kitchen and dining room. Esther stopped to admire the cabinets that Paul had built. He was slowly remodeling the kitchen during his off time.

"It's really looking good, Paul," she enthused. "I can't wait to see how it looks when you're completely finished."

Esther looked back into the living room to see if Ninja was following them, but didn't see the K9.

"Where's Ninja?" she asked her brother.

Paul just grinned at his sister and motioned her toward the breakfast bar. He handed her a plate of sandwiches to carry to the table while he brought the chips and tea. Esther shrugged and grabbed the plate.

Half-way to the table, Esther felt a cold nose touch the back of her leg. She jumped and almost dropped the sandwiches. Paul burst out laughing as his sister whirled around and saw Ninja standing directly behind her.

"Ninja! I didn't even hear you!"

Paul nodded enthusiastically.

"It's a new trick I taught him. Remember when I bent over to whisper in his ear? I told him 'stealth' and he knew to wait until you wouldn't see him, then sneak up behind you."

"For heaven's sake, why did you teach him that?" Esther demanded. "I just about jumped out of my skin."

"Well, it is great for doing that to bratty sisters," Paul chuckled. "But I think it may also be useful in our job. I'll have to see how and when I can use it."

"Was he able to use it on the job?"

Stephen was curious.

"He couldn't really tell me about open cases, but he did tell me that Ninja caused quite a few drug dealers and crooks to jump just like I did. I've even used it in the classroom a few times. When I have a student that needs extra watching, I tell Ninja "stealth and guard" and point to the student. He waits until the child is engaged somewhere else and then quietly follows him to make sure he stays out of trouble."

Stephen shook his head in admiration.

"That's great! You never know when you might need a German Shepherd in stealth mode."

Chapter 10

Stephen stepped into the restaurant and paused a moment to let his eyes adjust from the bright sunlight to the dim lights inside. He looked around with interest. The smells coming from the kitchen made his stomach growl. It seemed like it had been a long time since breakfast.

"Stephen! Over here!"

Scott Donaldson waved to Stephen from a booth in the corner. Stephen swiftly wove through the tables to shake his friend's hand. Scott grabbed his hand and then pulled Stephen into a bear hug, pounding on his friend's back as his face glowed.

"You're looking good, man," he enthused. "How's life treating you?"

Stephen grinned at him.

"Not bad, how about you? You enjoying married life? Looks like Lisa is feeding you well."

Stephen poked his friend's round belly. Scott had been slightly overweight since Stephen had known him, but it looked like his friend had gained another ten pounds or so.

"Feeds me like a king," Scott boasted. "You ever think about settling down? Got that 'special someone' in your life yet?"

Stephen smiled, thinking about Esther.

"Yeah, maybe," he hedged. "We're still at the point of friendship."

"Better get on the ball, buddy," Scott advised. "You ain't getting any younger." The waitress came over and took their orders. Stephen ordered a grilled chicken club with fries and a large coffee. Scott ordered the same thing and then added a side of fried chicken tenders and a milkshake. Stephen just shook his head.

"What?" Scott protested. "I have to keep my strength up. I just came from my checkup at the VA hospital. Man, they checked everything! About wore me out!"

Stephen looked concerned. "Are you okay? Anything to worry about?"

Scott looked sheepish. "I'm good, except for my weight and cholesterol."

He saw Stephen about to comment on his eating and headed him off.

"I don't eat like this all the time," he offered. "I'm celebrating surviving my check up and seeing my old friend."

When their food arrived, the two concentrated on eating for a few minutes. After enjoying half of his sandwich and fries, Stephen paused to take a long drink of coffee.

"I haven't seen you in over a year, Scott. So, what's happening in your part of the woods?" he queried his friend. It didn't matter how long the two were separated, they always picked up right where they left off.

Scott was from Forrestville but had moved to a small town near Longview. Although there was a VA clinic in Longview, Scott preferred the main hospital in Shreveport, claiming there was more to do in Shreveport/Bossier when he finished his appointments.

"Not much," Scott munched on another chicken tender for minute, chewing slowly and thoughtfully.

"I saw another one of our fine Forrestville citizens back in June."

"Oh yeah? Who was it?"

Stephen was busy finishing off his sandwich while he listened to his friend.

"The guy that owns all those businesses in Forrestville."

Scott slurped the rest of his milkshake until Stephen was ready to snatch the cup away.

"Scott! Please stop that racket."

Stephen glared at his friend. He couldn't stand that slurping sound.

"You'll need to be more specific. We have several business owners in our charming little town."

"I think his name is . . ., um, I think . . . Well, dang, I can't think of his name.

"Well, that's helpful."

Stephen was only mildly curious. There were several men in Forrestville who owned multiple businesses and even a couple who did business all over the world. He idly wondered why these men even lived in a small town like Forrestville.

"Yeah, well, whoever it was. I saw him at the ER when I had to go in because of an allergic reaction."

"I'm sorry you had to go in. What were you allergic to?"

"Tomatoes. Made me break out in a rash."

Scott reached over and snagged one of Stephen's fries.

"Anyway, this guy comes in with his right arm looking pretty rough. It looked like something had chewed on it. The towel he was holding on it was bloody."

Now Stephen was very interested.

"What do you think happened?" he prodded Scott to go on.

Scott was into his story now.

"Well he came into the waiting area at the Longview ER with that chewed-up looking arm and saw me looking at him. At first, I think he wanted to tell me to mind my own business, but then he smiled at me and told me he had mistakenly teased a friend's dog and the dog had attacked him. I thought the story sounded kind of funny, but hey, stranger things have happened."

"Yeah, stranger things," Stephen answered distractedly. He was thinking about the timing. That was when Paul Daniels had been shot. Was it just a coincidence, or something else?

Chapter 11

"Hi Esther!"

Dr. Harris's veterinary assistant, Jennifer, came out from behind the counter and greeted Esther as she and Ninja came in. The young woman stroked Ninja's back as the German Shepherd stood, his beautiful tail drooping.

"Poor fellow, he hates coming to the vet, doesn't he?"

Esther stroked her dog's back.

"He's had a rough time of it since the shooting, so I guess he has a good reason."

When Jennifer saw Esther fighting tears, she enveloped her in a comforting hug.

"I guess you've had a rough time too."

She gave Esther another squeeze and scratched Ninja behind the ears.

"Dr. Harris will be with you in a few minutes."

While Esther and Ninja waited for the vet, they watched a young family with a small Border Collie mix. The two little girls were taking the dog through all of its tricks. The oldest one looked up and saw Esther.

"Miss Daniels!"

She squealed and bounced over to where Esther sat, dragging her sister with her.

"Chelly, this is my teacher, Miss Daniels."

The younger girl rolled her eyes and answered her sister saucily, "I know who your teacher is. You don't have to tell me every time, Annie!"

Their mother just looked at them and shook her head, sharing an amused smile with Esther.

"Annie, is that your little dog that you've been telling me so much about?"

Annie's face brightened. "She's the smartest dog in the world!" The child shot an apologetic look at Ninja. "Sorry, Ninja. You're the second smartest dog!"

"Well, that's quite a statement, young lady. Why don't you show me?"

Annie and Chelly called their dog over.

"C'mere Nikki!"

The little dog trotted over and the two dogs introduced themselves with a little sniffing. When they were both satisfied with their introductions, the girls proceeded to show off their dog.

"Watch this, Miss Daniels, Nikki knows sign language."

Chelly put up her first two fingers on each hand and put one on top of the other. Nikki sat when she saw the gesture.

"That's the sign for sit. She also knows the sign for speak."

Chelly circled her right index finger in front of her mouth and Nikki barked.

Annie took over showing off their dog.

"This one is our favorite. Nikki, what do you do when you're on fire?"

The little dog lay down and rolled over.

Esther was impressed.

"That's great, girls! You taught her to stop, drop, and roll. Maybe you can be dog trainers when you grow up."

Chelly nodded. "I'm going to have a Golden Retriever when I grow up and I'm going to teach her how to talk!"

Before Esther could answer, Jennifer called for her and Ninja.

"Goodbye girls. Goodbye Nikki. You really are one smart dog."

She waved to the girls' mother and led Ninja to the back.

Esther stroked Ninja's head and spoke softly to him as the veterinary assistant prepped him for his teeth cleaning.

"The sedative we gave him should be taking effect soon, then you can leave him with us."

Esther nodded as she struggled to hide the tears in her eyes. Even a routine event, like a teeth cleaning, caused her concern for her dog. She knew things could go wrong while he was under the general anesthesia. Ninja had become more than just her brother's dog. He was her friend and companion.

The assistant laid a hand on Esther's shoulder.

"It's okay," she reassured her. "I know it's hard to see your pet like that."

Esther smiled gratefully. "I feel foolish getting so wrought up about something this simple." She dug in her purse in a futile search for a tissue.

"I guess I'm just sentimental about him."

"Hey, you don't have to apologize to me for that." The assistant grinned at her as she handed Esther several tissues.

"I get choked up about all of our animals. Don't worry, we'll take good care of him. Are you sure you don't want to leave him overnight?"

"I actually thought about it for a whole two seconds, and then decided against it. I don't think he's quite ready for an overnight stay. I'll just sit in the waiting area and grade papers." She patted her satchel. "With a class the size of mine, I'll be busy for quite a while. He'll probably be ready to go before I am!"

"Frank, why are we fooling around with someone's gas heater? We don't know anything about working with natural gas."

Jesse fidgeted in his seat. Something didn't seem right to him.

"Hey, man, just relax. I know what I'm doing. I used to work with a gas company in Shreveport."

Frank glanced at Jesse, then back at the street.

"I'll show you what you need to do."

"But, we're groundskeepers, not utility workers. I still don't understand . . ."

Frank pulled over and put the van in Park, then turned to face Jesse. His face was hard and his tone was cold.

"You need to learn something about this job, Jesse. Sometimes you just have to keep your mouth shut and do what you're told. We were given an assignment and that's what we're going to do."

Jesse stared at his friend suspiciously. Why wouldn't Frank answer his questions about what they were doing? He started to object when his phone rang. The screen showed the number for his next-door neighbor. Jesse felt a frisson of anxiety as he answered the call. Mrs. Suttles wouldn't call just to chat. Something was wrong.

"Hello?"

"Jesse, is that you? This is Mrs. Suttles."

"What's wrong?"

"I went over to your house to visit with Abigail and found her out cold on the floor. She was hardly breathing!"

The elderly woman sounded like she was in tears.

"The ambulance came and took your aunt to Forrestville General Hospital."

Jesse felt cold all over. He managed to thank her although he could barely talk, then ended the call.

""Frank, that was our neighbor. Aunt Abigail is in the hospital. I have to go home to get my truck and get to the hospital."

Frank shook his head. "No way, man, we got a job to do and we're going to do it."

"Come on, Frank, this is my aunt! She raised me. I need to be there for her like she's been there for me."

Frank considered for a minute, then sighed.

"Okay, I might as well take you home. You won't be any good to me if you're thinking about being somewhere else."

He made a quick turn, then looked over at Jesse.

"But you owe me big time, dude. If the boss finds out, he won't be happy with either one of us."

Jesse sagged in relief. If he had had to, he would have just jumped out of the van when it stopped and hoofed it home. That would have taken him a long time.

"Thanks, Frank. I won't forget this, man."

"You got that right. I won't let you forget."

"Mr. Williams, I won't lie to you. Your aunt is in very serious condition."

The ER doctor looked compassionately at the young man. Frank had dropped Jesse off at home and gone back to work. Jesse had jumped in his truck and broken all speed limits on his way to the hospital. He had arrived breathless and frantic for news about his aunt.

"What's wrong with her?"

Jesse was terrified. Aunt Abigail was the only family he had left.

"We're still running tests, but we know for sure she has pneumonia. Might have had it for quite a while before she passed out."

Jesse remembered that his aunt had seemed more tired than usual and had been coughing for the past several weeks. Every time he asked her about the cough, she would pass it off as "still getting over that bronchitis." He knew she didn't like going to the doctor, so he didn't push. Now he wished he had. Maybe she wouldn't be here now if he had insisted she go back to her doctor.

"Will she be okay? Can I go see her?"

Jesse didn't realize how young and frightened he sounded.

"We're doing everything we can for her. Come on, I'll walk you down there."

The ER doctor put a reassuring hand on Jesse's shoulder. Normally, Jesse would have shrugged it off or backed away. He had a large personal space and didn't allow just anyone to touch him. Right now, though, that hand was comforting to Jesse.

Abigail Matthews was a slender woman whose frail appearance hid a strong personality. She was kind and compassionate, but could become firm and no-nonsense in a heartbeat, when necessary. Now she seemed even more frail as she lay in the hospital bed surrounded by equipment designed to keep her alive.

Jesse approached her bed slowly and quietly so he would not wake her. He looked around for a chair that he could pull up to her bed so he could sit with her.

"You can stop sneaking around, young man," Abigail murmured as she struggled to open her eyes. "Even asleep, I can still hear you."

Her nephew had to smile even as his heart was breaking at seeing her this vulnerable. He never had been able to sneak past her. A tear slid down his cheek as he cupped her hand in both of his.

"How are you feeling, Aunt Ab?"

"Don't cry, sweetheart," she managed to look up into his troubled eyes.

"Your old auntie's going to be alright. I just need to rest and get a little medicine, that's all. These nice people here are taking good care of me. Why, I might get so spoiled, you won't be able to stand me when I get home."

Abigail stopped to cough, a deep wracking sound that twisted Jesse's heart. When she motioned for a drink he hurried to pour her some water and lift her up so she could take a few sips.

Jesse tried to laugh.

"You're not old, Aunt Ab. And, I bet you'll be finding ways to take care of these people before you get out of here."

He tucked her hand back inside the hospital bed and turned to leave.

"They said not to stay too long, so I'm going to go so you can start working on getting well. You take a nice nap and I'll be back later for another visit."

Abigail watched her nephew as he walked out of her room. She understood his fear at finding her in the hospital. But she sensed there was another burden on him.

"I need to have a talk with him," she murmured to herself as she began to feel drowsy again. "Next time he visits."

With that she closed her eyes and surrendered to sleep.

Frank parked down the street from Esther's house and jumped out of the panel truck. Some careful detailing had changed it to look like a city utility vehicle. Frank wore dark blue trousers and a light blue shirt so he would look like one of the local gas company employees. He made a show of knocking on the door and calling out "Gas company!" before he pulled on a pair of latex gloves, jimmied the lock and entered the house.

Just inside the door he stopped and looked around the house to locate the gas heater. Even though the weather was still mild, he knew people would be calling to have their heaters and gas fireplaces checked before the first cold snap. Jesse had told him that his aunt had called the gas company the week before.

Thinking about Jesse made Frank shake his head. He was a good guy, but the kid was too soft as far as Frank was concerned. He just didn't understand that you have to look out for yourself first.

Frank tiptoed over to the heater and fumbled to get the grille off the unit. Working swiftly, he made a few adjustments, then cleaned up and put the grille back in place. He pulled the door open and reached back around to lock it, making sure as he closed the door that he looked as if he was supposed to be there. Then he walked briskly back to the truck and drove a block or two up the street.

About five minutes later, Esther's little blue sedan and Stephen's silver SUV turned the corner and pulled into her driveway.

Frank couldn't help the smug smile that spread across his face. After tonight, that woman and her dog would not be a problem anymore.

Chapter 12

Stephen groaned loudly as he carried Ninja to the door. Esther hurried ahead of him to open the door and turn on the lights.

"You can put him on his bed in the living room. I want to keep an eye on him for a while before we go to bed."

Esther looked apologetically at Stephen.

"I'm sorry about cancelling out on you for the concert. I just can't bring myself to leave him alone and David and Christy are at the concert. I hate that you missed it too."

Stephen shook his head. "Don't worry about it."

"Yeah, but you told me you've had tickets for that concert for months!" He carefully laid Ninja on the dog bed, then turned to Esther, taking both of her hands in his. "Like I said, don't worry about it. I'd rather be here with you and Ninja any time."

Esther gazed into his intense brown eyes for a minute. Flustered at the tenderness she saw there, she stepped back, pulling her hands from his light clasp.

Seeing Esther's discomfort at the look that had passed between them, Stephen made a big show of rubbing his back.

"Esther, I think you're feeding him too much. That dog weighs a ton!"

Esther grinned gratefully and answered him impishly. "Nah, just a half-ton."

She moved toward the kitchen. "Would you like a cup of coffee before you go? It will only take a few minutes to fix."

Stephen's face lit up.

"Sure! Do you have any cookies? I love your chocolate chip cookies!"

Esther thought about teasing about feeding him too much, but one look at his trim build and well-developed muscles changed her mind. She hurried to the coffee pot and started fixing their snack. She was alarmed at how often she had been noticing how attractive Stephen was.

"Just friends," she reminded herself.

It was getting harder for her to remember that.

When the coffee was ready, she fixed a tray with coffee and cookies for both of them and carried it into the living room. When Stephen offered to carry it for her, she declined.

"Can't have you doing any more heavy lifting," she teased. "It might mess up your back."

Stephen groaned theatrically, playing up the "bad back."

Esther just laughed at him and handed him his coffee and the plate of her famous cookies. Stephen eagerly accepted the plate and with an impish grin chose three of the largest cookies.

Ninja wearily lifted his head for a moment to watch them. Then he turned to look around the house. He sniffed the air and tried to snarl and bark but it came out more like a grunt.

Esther hurried to his side and stroked the dog's head.

"What's wrong, boy?" she asked. "Is that sedative making you feel tired?"

Ninja growled again and then lay down, his eyes drooping shut.

Esther and Stephen sat in companionable silence for a few minutes as they enjoyed their cookies and coffee. Then Esther thought about a question that had been nagging at her.

"You seem to have a good relationship with our police chief; like you've known her for a long time."

Stephen looked up with a sad smile.

"Not really a long time, but I met her at a very hard time in my life."

At Esther's questioning look, Stephen sighed and shook his head.

"It's hard to talk about it," he admitted. "I was engaged several years ago to a wonderful woman named Renee."

Esther was stunned. She had had no clue that Stephen had been engaged. She didn't want to interrupt him though, so she just smiled sympathetically and nodded her head to encourage him to go on.

"One night we were supposed to go out to eat, but I had caught a bad cold. I'm afraid I'm a big baby when I get sick and I made a big deal about needing certain groceries to help me 'survive' my illness. Renee tucked me into my recliner and then drove to our local supermarket to pick up my groceries for me. When she headed back to her car, she was robbed at gunpoint by some thug who probably wanted the money for drugs."

Stephen stopped and drew in a ragged breath. It took him a minute to be able to go on.

"The security videos showed that even though she fully cooperated, he shot her in cold blood and left her to die in the parking lot. Because it was late in the evening, no one witnessed the robbery or the murder."

"Where does Police Chief Jones come in?" Esther interrupted. Her heart ached for Stephen. She could see the murder of his fiancée still deeply affected him.

"Maggie was the homicide detective that worked the case."

Stephen got up and paced behind the couch, then sat back down.

"She was very thorough and professional in her investigation and caught the perpetrator a few weeks later. She was also very gentle and supportive with me. Maggie is a tough investigator, but she has a heart for the victims as well. Since then, we've stayed in touch. I was really glad when I found out she had taken the job of police chief in Forrestville."

Esther slid closer to Stephen and laid her hand on his arm. When he looked down into her eyes, she looped her arm through his.

"I'm so sorry you had to go through that, Stephen. She must have been a wonderful woman to be engaged to a special guy like you."

Stephen smiled sadly and stood.

"I guess I better get going so you two can get some rest."

Esther walked with him to the door.

Suddenly Stephen put his arms around Esther and pulled her to him for a hug. Esther hesitated a moment and then put her arms around him. He held her gently for a moment and then tilted her chin up and brushed a kiss across her lips. It was just a brief touch to her mouth but Esther felt it all the way to her toes.

"Thanks, Esther. You're a pretty special person yourself."

Stephen cupped her cheek in his hand for a moment, then stepped away.

"Pleasant dreams."

Esther barely managed to tell him good night. She was in shock over the kiss. Part of her wanted to hold that kiss to her heart and see where things would go. Part of her was terrified to allow herself to fall in love with Stephen.

She locked the door and then went around the house making sure everything was secure. After changing into her pajamas and brushing her teeth, Esther settled on the couch with a pillow and afghan. She decided she would leave Ninja where he was and just sleep on the couch that night. It was a comfortable sofa and she had spent many a night there. Esther made sure she had her phone nearby and then snuggled in and went to sleep with a soft smile on her lips.

She didn't even notice the faint odor of gas that had begun to permeate the house.

Chapter 13

Stephen felt like his emotions were on a roller coaster as he drove home. He had not planned to kiss Esther, especially after such a serious discussion, but somehow it had seemed right at that moment.

When he arrived at his door, Stephen decided he was too keyed up to sleep, so he would go for a run. Changing to sweats and a t-shirt, he grabbed his keys and set out. After the exercise, he felt he had burned off some of his adrenaline.

As he walked in the door of his apartment, he looked across to his breakfast bar and saw he still had a couple of books that he had borrowed from Esther several weeks before and had intended to return that evening. Her call to help bring Ninja home had distracted him.

This was a perfect excuse to call her. He wanted to hear her voice one more time before he went to bed.

Stephen quickly showered and changed to clean sweats and t-shirt, then settled on his bed to call Esther. As he dialed her number, Stephen glanced at his bedside clock. It was only 9:30, so hopefully she would still be awake.

"Hello?"

Esther's voice sounded groggy. Stephen winced. He hadn't thought about her going to bed early.

"Hey, Esther, it's me, Stephen. I'm sorry I woke you up. I'll call you back tomorrow."

Esther mumbled back to him.

"What did you say?"

He started to feel a sliver of worry. Something didn't sound right in her voice.

"I said that's okay. I'm just . . ."

Esther's voice trailed away.

"I have a pounding headache," she complained. "I'm going back to bed."

Stephen heard the phone drop without being disconnected.

"Esther? Esther!"

Stephen felt a sense of urgency remembering the section about natural gas in the home safety seminar he took two weeks ago.

He grabbed his keys and headed to his car.

"Sweetheart, hold on. I'm coming!" he yelled into his phone. He disconnected so he could dial 911. After explaining the situation and giving Esther's address, he threw his phone in the passenger seat and pointed his car toward Esther's house.

On the way he lifted his heart in a fervent prayer.

"Please let me be in time. Lord, I can't lose another woman I care about."

Esther heard pounding and Stephen's voice yelling for her to open the door. She struggled to get up, but felt woozy and disoriented. She could see Ninja's limp body sprawled on his bed. Esther heard the shattering of glass as Stephen broke the window beside the front door. Then Stephen was lifting her in his arms and carrying her outside.

She felt the cool smoothness of leather as he laid her in the back seat of his SUV. A few moments later she heard the hatch open in the back. She could hear Stephen grunt as he eased Ninja into the back. After a few minutes, she felt Stephen's hand holding hers, the other one smoothing her hair away from her face.

"Hang on honey, help is on the way."

"Ninja?"

Esther tried to lift her head to look for her dog.

"I got him. He's lying in the back of my SUV."

The redness of Esther's cheeks confirmed Stephen's fears. She had carbon monoxide poisoning. Ninja had it too – the big dog was completely limp. He checked the shepherd and found him barely breathing.

Stephen couldn't help wondering how this happened. He knew Esther had checked all of her gas appliances just a couple weeks earlier to ensure everything was in good working order. She said her parents had taught her to do that several times a year to make sure there were no problems with water or gas leaks.

He thought about the panel truck he had seen parked a block away from Esther's house. What was that truck doing there so late in the day?

The sound of the sirens pulled Stephen from his musing. He couldn't help feeling that, right now, those sirens must be one of the most beautiful sounds in the world.

He led the paramedics to where he had laid Esther and Ninja, and watched as the EMT's took over with them. Once he knew Esther and Ninja were in good hands, Stephen spoke with the fire captain about his suspicions.

Quickly Stephen explained about Esther's diligent maintenance of her appliances and the panel truck that had been parked nearby. The fire captain nodded as he listened.

"Good work, Mr. Abrams. I'm glad you got here so quickly. We'll check things out."

Stephen thanked him, then swung his gaze over to where the paramedics were checking on Esther. They had strapped her to a gurney and placed an oxygen mask on her.

He hurried to the ambulance and was immensely relieved to see that although Esther still looked a little woozy, she seemed to be doing better with the oxygen.

She looked around for Ninja.

"Where's Ninja?" she tried to say.

One of the paramedics reached over and adjusted her oxygen mask.

"Leave that on please," he said, smiling reassuringly. "My partner is checking out your dog."

"Stephen, check on Ninja please?"

Esther's voice was muffled by the oxygen mask, but Stephen heard her and saw the plea in her eyes.

"I'll go check on him right now. Just lay still and rest."

Stephen walked around to where the other paramedic was checking out the shepherd.

"How's the dog?" he asked quietly. "The lady is very anxious to make sure he's okay."

The other paramedic shook his head.

"It was close," he said. "I'd feel better if a veterinarian could check him out."

Stephen looked back at the ambulance where Esther was anxiously trying to see where Ninja was.

"What can I tell her?"

"Just tell her he's okay but needs to be checked out by his vet. She really needs to go to the hospital herself. They'll want to check her oxygen and hemoglobin levels there."

The fire captain caught Stephen's eye and motioned him over to give him an update.

"Mr. Abrams, we've gotten the gas turned off to the house and done a preliminary investigation. It does look as if someone tampered with her heater so that the gas turned on but not the flame. It would be best if she stayed somewhere else for a few days. I've notified the police chief and we'll investigate this more thoroughly."

Stephen felt sick inside. If he had not called Esther when he did, he would not have known she was in trouble. If he had not gotten here in time, she could have died. Nodding to the fire captain, he pulled his cell phone from his pocket and quickly dialed a number.

"David? Can you and Christy meet me at Forrestville General?"

He filled them in on what had happened.

"I think it would be a good idea if Esther had someone to stay with her at the hospital. I'm going to take Ninja to the vet's office. They'll also need somewhere to stay for a few days when they're released."

He heard David talking to Christy then coming back to the phone.

"They can stay with us," David reassured him. "We have plenty of room here."

Stephen sagged with relief.

"Great! Let me get Ninja taken care of and I'll meet you at the hospital."

As he put his phone in his pocket, Stephen felt a tap on his shoulder. He turned around and saw the local veterinarian standing behind him.

"Dr. Harris! What are you doing here?"

He couldn't even begin to tell how glad he was to see the man.

"I live a few houses down," the veterinarian explained. "I stepped outside to take out the trash and saw the ambulance go by. When I saw it stop at Esther's house, I came over to see if I could help."

"You sure can."

He motioned for Dr. Harris to follow him over where Ninja was stretched out.

"This is Ninja's veterinarian," Stephen explained to the paramedic.

Dr. Harris leaned over Ninja and began a swift examination, quietly questioning the paramedic as he went. Then he stood and motioned to Stephen.

"Can you take Ninja and me back to my house?" he asked. "I can keep an eye on him there. I don't really want to traumatize him further by making him return to the clinic tonight. With everything he's been through, I'm afraid the poor dog does not have good memories of my clinic."

Stephen secured Ninja in the back of his vehicle and drove around to the veterinarian's home.

"Thanks, Dr. Harris," he said. "I'll let Esther know you have Ninja. She will be so relieved you didn't have to put him back in 'doggy hospital.'"

They shared a brief chuckle before Stephen pulled away.

As he sped to the hospital, Stephen lifted up a prayer for Esther and Ninja.

"And, Lord," he added, "thank You for getting me there in time."

He shook his head in wonder,

"I didn't think it was possible after losing Renee, but I love Esther so much. I don't want to lose her. I think she loves me too. She just doesn't know it yet."

Chapter 14

"Christy, thank you for staying at the hospital with me last night."

Esther shifted on the hospital bed as she smiled gratefully at her friend.

"I also appreciate your offering to let me stay at your place while my house is investigated and my heater repaired."

Esther rushed her next words, "But you don't have to do that. I can stay at a motel. I don't want to be any bother."

Christy gave her a warm smile.

"You are welcome and you are not a bother."

She found an extra pillow and put it behind Esther to help her sit up more comfortably.

"Sweetie, don't you know how much David and I love you? I can't wait for you to come spend some time with us."

She leaned over and lowered her voice conspiratorially.

"Maybe we can boot David out and have some girl time. Watch some chick flicks, eat chocolate, and run around in our jammies."

Esther laughed. "That sound great considering all I have with me are my jammies. They won't let me back in the house yet."

Christy's eyes sparkled.

"No problem, I think our girls left some clothes. Something in there ought to fit you. If not, we can stop at one of the shops and pick up a couple outfits for you."

She stopped for a moment and tapped her chin, then looked at Esther with a mischievous twinkle.

"Come to think of it, Joy's Dress Shop has a couple of real cute outfits that would be perfect on you. Since it's my idea, it will be my treat."

Esther looked like she was going to object, but Christy interrupted her.

"No argument, young lady. My girls are grown and moved away. I want the chance to spoil somebody for a little while and that somebody is you."

Esther looked away. She loved the idea of being spoiled, but she was afraid of spending too much time with the Michaels. They were friends of her family, but she was afraid to let them get any closer.

A few hours later the doctor on duty discharged Esther.

"I recommend you take it easy for a day or two," he cautioned.

"This is Saturday," Esther said. "Can I go back to work Monday? I really hate trying to find a substitute at this late date."

The doctor considered for a moment, then nodded.

"I think you'll be okay by then. Just go by how you feel. Be sure to follow up with your primary care doctor."

About that time, they heard toenails clicking down the hall outside and a knock on the door. Stephen stuck his head in the door.

"Can I come in?" he asked cheerfully. "I brought someone to see you."

Esther looked up and laughed as Ninja bounded through the door followed by Stephen and Maggie.

"Hey, buddy! I'm so glad to see you!"

Esther struggled with tears as she hugged her dog and stroked his back.

She looked up at Stephen.

"Is he really okay? What did the vet say?"

Stephen sat next to her on the hospital bed and put a comforting hand on hers. Maggie stepped over to chat with Christy for a moment.

"The vet said that he put Ninja on oxygen and IV fluids for a couple hours last night and that Ninja rested well and seemed much more like himself this morning. Ninja also seemed *very* glad he was at the vet's house instead of the clinic."

Esther quickly flipped the tears from her cheeks and gave Stephen a tremulous smile.

"That was really nice of him to take Ninja to his house last night."

She shook her finger at Ninja.

"I hope you were a well-behaved houseguest."

He barked and licked her finger.

Stephen laughed. "Dr. Harris didn't have any complaints this morning."

Maggie stepped over to stand by the bed, her expression grim.

"Esther, your gas heater was tampered with so that it would release the gas without the flame coming on. Do you know of anyone who would want to harm you, who has a grudge against you?"

Nausea swirled through her stomach as Esther felt darkness crowd the edge of her vision. Maggie's and Stephen's voices seemed to come from far away.

Stephen slid his arm around her and gave her a gentle shake, alarmed at her pallor and shallow breathing.

"Esther, come on, honey. Breathe!"

She forced herself to breathe deeply. After a few moments Esther was able to speak.

"No, I can't think of anyone who would want to kill me, or even why!"

Esther shuddered.

"I can't think of anyone who would hate me that much or who would gain anything from my death."

As she spoke Esther remembered Kenneth Owens and wondered if the hatred he felt for Paul was so great that he would try to kill Paul's sister and dog, even though Paul was gone now. She realized Stephen was talking and turned her attention back to him.

"Could it be someone that Paul arrested?" Stephen suggested. "Maybe this person doesn't know that Paul is dead and thought he could get even with your brother by killing you."

"Well, there is someone." Esther hesitated. "I don't know, though if I should say anything."

"If you have someone in mind, you need to tell me."

Maggie watched Esther intently.

"Even if it's just a hint of suspicion, I need to know."

Esther told her about Ken Owens and the threat to Paul after Jimmy Owens committed suicide.

Maggie nodded. "Yeah, we all knew about his threats. I might need to have a little talk with Mr. Owens."

"But I'm not accusing him of anything!" Esther protested. She didn't want Ken Owens to think she had sent Maggie to him.

Esther stood carefully and looked around the circle of friends in her hospital room.

"I don't think I should go to the Michaels," she declared. "I don't want to put them in danger."

Christy stepped forward. "Honey, you don't need to worry about us. David and I are both crack shots. We know how to take care of ourselves, and our friends."

"We'll also be keeping an eye on you," Maggie offered. "I'll order extra patrols near the Michaels' place."

The three friends watched as Esther struggled with her decision. Her need for independence was well-known. In fact, Stephen was surprised that Esther had even let him help with Ninja after the dog's dental cleaning.

Christy took the initiative. She stepped up to her friend and lifted Esther's chin so that their eyes met.

"Esther, you can't keep pushing away the people who care for you. We want to help you because we love you. Besides, I'm looking forward to our girls' night. You can't cheat me out of that now."

Esther took a deep breath and nodded.

"Okay, I'll go for now."

She looked at them almost fiercely.

"But only for a couple days. Then I want to go home."

"But, Esther," Stephen started to object.

Maggie caught his eye and shook her head. She recognized the glint in Christy's eye and knew Christy would have a heart-to-heart talk with Esther. Her friend would get to the bottom of Esther's tendency to push people away when they started to get close.

When Esther was ready to leave, the floor nurse arrived with a wheelchair.

"Good morning, my name is Julie. I'm here to take you to the door."

"Is the wheelchair really necessary?" Esther protested. "I feel fine and I'm perfectly capable of walking on my own."

The nurse gave her patient a stern look, then smiled and winked.

"Sorry, but it's hospital policy. We have to see you to the door in our fine conveyance."

Stephen helped Esther into the chair, then asked Julie to allow him to push Esther's chair. "I promise we won't go racing down the hall."

Julie laughed and waved him to the wheelchair's handles. Stephen put his hands on them to push, but couldn't resist adding racing noises as they moved down the hallway. The women just laughed at his foolishness.

As they approached the sliding doors, Jesse came hurrying in, looking worried. He stopped short when he saw Esther in the wheelchair. His face paled; then he tried to walk past them.

"Jesse, what are you doing here? Is everything okay?"

"I'm sorry, Esther, but I need to go on up and see Aunt Abigail before I go to work."

Jesse wouldn't look Esther in the eye.

"Abigail is in the hospital?" Esther was startled. "What's wrong?"

"She was found unconscious yesterday by our neighbor, Mrs. Suttles. When I got here last night, the doctor said she has pneumonia."

Esther's heart went out to the young man. She could see he was almost in tears.

"Please let us know if there is anything we can do to help," she offered. "We'll be praying for her."

"Thanks, Esther. I appreciate it."

Jesse strode away, but not before giving Esther a strangely guilty look.

Chapter 15

"I'm looking for your crusty old police chief," Stephen told the police officer who came forward to help him. He heard a sound between a snort and a laugh.

"Boy, I ought to arrest you for that!"

Police Chief Maggie Jones was lean and fit at 47, with shoulder length blond hair that she kept in a French braid when she was in uniform. She stepped over to Stephen, holding her handcuffs menacingly. The officers in the station watched the byplay with amusement.

"What are you going to arrest me for?" he baited her.

"How about being ugly?"

The two glared at each other for another moment, then broke out laughing.

"Stephen, don't you have anything better to do with your day than to come in here and insult your friendly police chief?"

Maggie shook her head at him.

"Come on back to my office. Can't have you cluttering up the front and getting in the way."

The police chief led the way into her office and offered Stephen a bottle of water from her mini fridge. Stephen opened it and took a long drink, then recapped it and set the bottle down.

"Okay, what's on your mind? I know you didn't come in just to chat with your old pal."

Stephen looked around her office a moment while he organized his thoughts. It was clean but slightly cluttered with papers on her desk, a baseball and bat in the corner, no doubt left by her son, and photographs and diplomas lining the walls.

"Maggie, you know about the incidents that have happened to Esther Daniels?"

She nodded and motioned for him to continue.

"I'm not so sure those are all accidents or just random incidents. I think someone is trying to kill Esther."

Stephen had a hard time voicing the words. He had been quietly asking around town about who saw what. Stephen had a knack for getting people to tell him what he wanted to know without actually coming out and asking. The things he had been hearing formed a picture in his mind that was alarming.

"I've suspected as much. Tell me why you think so."

Maggie's voice was low and commanding. That was part of why she was such a good investigator. She knew how to listen first, then act.

Stephen told her about his discussions with townspeople who had seen someone in Mr. Winchell's car a few minutes before it rolled down the hill toward Esther and Ninja.

"Did they say who it was?"

Maggie leaned forward.

"No one could agree on who they saw there. I'm surprised someone didn't say they saw Elvis or Bigfoot."

Stephen's attempt at humor felt awkward to him. Maggie just smiled briefly, then nodded for him to continue his narrative.

"You know that when Esther's gas heater malfunctioned, the fire chief said it looked like someone had tampered with it. But, the next day, it was back to normal. I think someone slipped into the house while Esther had Ninja at the vet and tampered with the furnace. The next day that person, or someone working with him, slipped back in and put it back to normal."

"First of all, why were you in her house during an investigation? Second, do you have proof of any of this?"

Stephen sighed in frustration.

"No, just bits and pieces picked up here and there."

Maggie sat back and smiled at him.

"That's why I'm the police chief and you're a history teacher. I'm trained in investigative procedures. You're not."

"I also had an interesting conversation with a friend of mine."

Stephen recounted Scott's story about a Forrestville businessman at the emergency room in Longview the same day as Paul's murder.

"He said the man's arm looked like something had chewed on him. The businessman told him he had teased a friend's dog and it had attacked him."

Maggie's eyes narrowed slightly as Stephen described what his friend had seen.

"That is very interesting," she commented, "but, one, it's hearsay, and two, I can't do much without a name. I'll keep it in mind while we're investigating, though."

"There's something else."

Stephen ground his teeth together as he remembered seeing Frank watching Esther and her reaction when he tried to get her to understand that the man could be following her.

Maggie watched him with concern.

"What is it?"

"I'm pretty sure Frank Parker is following Esther," he blurted out.

He felt foolish now. Stephen knew he didn't have any proof that Frank meant Esther any harm, but it seemed so strange to him that Frank was often nearby when Esther and Stephen were in town.

"Stephen?"

Maggie leaned forward, her office chair squeaking.

"Why do you think Frank Parker is following Esther?" she prodded.

Stephen told her about the incident in town when Ninja had seen Frank and snarled at him. He left out the part about their argument.

Maggie got up and came around to where Stephen was pacing, stopping him with a hand on his arm.

"Stephen, I don't want you to get hurt trying to investigate, okay? We are still looking into Paul's death."

Her eyes grew steely.

"You can bet we're still investigating that. We're also checking into . . . some other things happening around town. Things I'm not at liberty to discuss with you."

Maggie leaned against her desk.

"If you see or hear something you think will help, we welcome your information."

Here the police chief stood straight, then leaned forward.

"But let me emphasize, you are *not* trained in these procedures! Let my officers and me do our jobs."

Stephen gazed at her steadily for a minute, his brown eyes intense.

"Maggie, I get what you're saying."

Now it was his turn to lean forward in emphasis.

"But I will not stand by and watch the woman I love be terrorized and killed. So, I will continue to keep my eyes and ears open. And, if necessary, ask my own questions."

Maggie shook her head.

"Stephen, you and I have known each other since we lived in Shreveport and I worked on Renee's case."

Stephen looked down, his jaw working. After five years, he still hurt at the memory of Renee's murder.

Maggie touched his arm briefly and brought his attention back to her.

"You still blame yourself, don't you?"

"Renee was at the supermarket that night buying groceries for me! If I had been with her, or if she had just stayed with me, none of that would have happened. You told me yourself that he probably targeted her because she was alone."

"Stephen, you know full well the evil that people can do. It was not your fault."

She stopped and smiled at him, her eyes twinkling.

"Did you just say you will not watch the woman you *love* be terrorized?"

Stephen paused a moment and smiled.

"Yeah, I did."

He caught Maggie's smirk and shook his head.

"You're just trying to change the subject. I still blame myself for Renee's death. I don't want to see Esther hurt."

Stephen tossed the empty water bottle in the trash can by Maggie's desk.

"I'll let you know if I hear anything."

As Stephen strode out of her office, Maggie Jones sat back in her chair and stared at the door. She smiled to herself.

"It's about time that boy fell in love again."

She stood up and walked out to the main lobby of the police station.

"Linda," she told her receptionist. "Get me the file on Paul Daniels' murder. I'd like to look at a couple of things."

The pretty young receptionist searched through the file cabinet for a moment then produced a thick file folder. She handed it to Maggie.

"Do you think you will find something that will finally close that case?" she asked her boss.

Maggie just smiled at the young woman.

"Your phone is ringing,"

As the receptionist hurried to answer the phone, Maggie took the folder into her office. After thinking for a moment, she returned to the file cabinet in the front office. Waving off Linda's offer to help, she pulled out the record of Paul's arrests and returned to her desk.

Maggie grabbed her bottle of water, took a small sip, then set it down without looking. She stared at the two files on her desk as if she could see the answers through the covers. She had a gut feeling they were right in front of her in those two folders. Praying for guidance, Maggie dove into the records, searching for the crucial element in both cases.

About an hour later Maggie looked up in satisfaction. She had found the threats made by Kenneth Owens. She also had found the list of evidence that Paul and the others on the team had found against Jimmy. Maggie knew that the team believed that Jimmy was just a henchman. There was someone who was in charge of the whole operation. They couldn't find evidence as to who that man was, but they had found evidence that pointed to several local businessmen, Ken Owens among them. There was not enough there to build a case, but it had provided a starting place.

Maggie leaned back in her chair and tapped her finger on her chin. This was very interesting, she thought. Things just might start coming together to solve Paul's murder and the drug ring they had been trying to break up for a long time.

"Jesse, Frank, I'd like to see you in my office."

The two men looked at each other uneasily and then filed into their employer's imposing home office.

The man they worked for settled himself into his office chair and waved them to the seats in front of his desk. Although his movements were gracious, they could see a steely glint in his eyes that did not bode well for them.

"Frank, I gave you an assignment," he started. "It should have been an easy assignment – kill Esther Daniels and her dog. Make sure it looks like an accident."

He stared at Frank until his henchman began to squirm.

"You have tried three times, and three times you have failed."

"It's not my fault," Frank started to object, but his boss cut him off.

"No excuses!"

The boss fixed his cold eyes on Frank.

"Kill the woman and her dog. I don't care how you do it – just do it!"

"Yessir! I will, sir."

Frank started to get up to leave, then looked back at the man behind the desk for permission. The big man nodded once. As Frank went out the door, Jesse started to follow him.

"One moment, Jesse."

The boss' voice was almost friendly.

Fear turned Jesse's stomach into a cauldron of acid. Nausea threatened as he turned back to his employer. He swallowed hard.

"Yes, sir?"

He tried to hide the trembling in his hands by holding them behind his back. The boss smiled, as if enjoying Jesse's discomfiture.

"Lately I've been sensing a lack of commitment on your part. I need to know I can count on you."

Jesse didn't know what to say. He couldn't promise he would do what the boss asked, not when his boss wanted him to commit murder.

"I'm trying my best, sir," he stammered.

The businessman studied Jesse with hooded eyes, as if weighing him. Finally, he waved Jesse away.

"Return to your duties. Make sure to clean up the driveway when you're done edging."

Jesse turned away, relieved. But he was stopped cold by his employer's next words.

"Be sure to give your aunt my regards."

Jesse finished loading the dishwasher and turned it on. As he wiped the counters his mind raced. He knew he had to get away from his boss and from his job, but how? He wasn't so much worried about his own safety as his aunt's. He knew his boss would not hesitate to hurt or even kill her if Jesse tried to quit.

Tears crowded the back of his eyes and his hands shook as he poured the coffee into the mugs and set them on the tray with the brownies from Mrs. Suttles. Jesse carefully wiped up the spill on the tray and tossed the paper towel in the trash.

"Jesse? Do you need any help, sweetheart?"

Aunt Abigail's voice was stronger than when she was in the hospital, but still sounded thin and frail to him.

"No, thanks, Aunt Abs. I got this." Jesse called to her. He shook himself mentally.

"Get a grip," he growled under his breath. He didn't want to burden his aunt with any of his problems. He wanted her concentrating on getting completely well.

Jesse pasted a smile on his face and carried the tray into the living room. He set the tray on the coffee table and handed his aunt her mug.

"Fresh hot coffee to go with fudgy homemade brownies," he chanted. "Just what the doctor ordered. Dr. Jesse that is!"

Abigail accepted the mug and took a cautious sip. "Ahhh, just right!"

She inhaled the aromas of coffee and chocolate wafting to her. Abigail carefully placed her coffee on the coaster on her side table, then chose a brownie. After enjoying a few bites of the treat, she set down her saucer and fixed her gaze on her nephew.

Jesse valiantly tried to look like he was enjoying his dessert, but he couldn't even taste the chocolate. His mind was filled with fear at what his boss might do to Aunt Abigail.

"You look like you're carrying the weight of the world on your shoulders," she commented. "Do you want to tell me about it?"

Jesse started. He shook his head, maybe a little too vigorously.

"Oh, no, Aunt Abigail. I'm fine."

"Jesse, I may be sick, but I'm not blind. I've been watching you for the past year. You have become increasingly moody and withdrawn."

Jesse tried to laugh, but it came out weak and pathetic. He hung his head, tears burning in his eyes. Finally, he nodded his head.

"Aunt Abigail, I'm in big trouble and I don't know what to do," he admitted.

Abigail gathered his hands in hers.

"Tell me about it."

"I don't want to burden you while you're sick," he began, but she interrupted him.

"Sweetheart, it will burden me more if you don't tell me. I'm alright. Please tell me what's bothering you."

Jesse sat quietly for a moment, trying to think how to tell this godly woman that he was selling drugs for a powerful and wealthy businessman. Bowing his head to avoid her eyes, he laid it all out – the drugs, the knowledge about Paul's murder and the attempts on Esther's and Ninja's lives. Jesse cried as he told her how many times he had tried to break away, but his boss had threatened to harm her.

Abigail's eyes glinted as she heard Jesse's story. Although disappointed in her nephew, she was more angry with the monster who employed him.

When Jesse finished, there was silence for a long moment. He hesitantly looked up into his aunt's eyes, expecting to see disapproval and disgust. Jesse feared she might even throw him out of the house. But instead he saw compassion. He wondered why he had never before realized the great love she had for him.

"Oh, Jesse!"

Abigail dropped his hands so she could envelop him in a hug.

"I'm so sorry you've gone through this alone. You should have come to me. "

"I couldn't, Aunt Abs," he replied. "He would have hurt you! I don't even know how I'll get away from him, now. But I have to! I can't stand working for him anymore!"

Abigail lifted her nephew's chin, meeting his miserable gaze with her determined one.

"We'll start with prayer," she told him. "That's first, last, and in-between everything we do. Then we'll wait for the Lord to tell us what to do. Until you hear from Him, just keep up your daily duties for the town. Is he still sending you out to deal drugs?"

Jesse shook his head.

"Not right now. We sold all of the last batch and he hasn't bought anymore yet."

Abigail nodded her head emphatically.

"Good! I hate for you to have to work for that thug a minute longer, but I guess it's necessary while we wait on the Lord to tell us what to do."

Jesse objected. "Aunt Abigail, he's a wealthy and well-known businessman."

"That doesn't matter!"

She cut him off.

"That just makes him a wealthy thug as far as I'm concerned. But God's been dealing with thugs for a long time. He'll know what to do."

Abigail took her nephew's hands again and bowed her head. Jesse clung to her hands in gratitude and desperation.

"Maybe she's right," he mused. "I sure can't do anything by myself. I need God to help me."

He bowed his head and lifted his own silent prayers, begging God to forgive him and clean up the mess he had made of his life.

Chapter 16

"Let's see,"

Christy looked over the spread of snacks on her coffee table.

"We have nachos, fried chicken, coffee, brownies, and M&M's. Oh yes, and strawberries and watermelon. Did I forget anything?"

Esther laughed at her friend.

"Yeah, the kitchen sink."

She leaned forward and snagged a nacho, being careful to get one loaded with cheese.

"Christy, is this a girls' night or a siege? There is no way we will be able to eat all of this tonight. We'd be sick if we tried."

"I'd be happy to help eat that," a voice offered.

"David!" Christy scolded. "You're supposed to be in your shop or the study. This is for girls only."

David just grinned and grabbed a handful of M&M's.

"I'm on my way out the door now," he promised. "Do you need anything before Ninja and I leave?"

Christy considered for a moment.

"Yes, I need one thing from you," she requested.

"And what would that be?" he inquired.

"A kiss."

"I think I can help with that."

Esther discreetly went to look at the movies she and Christy were planning to watch while the couple shared their tender moment. She felt wistful seeing the happy marriage the Michaels' shared and wondered if something like that could be in her future. She longed for it, yet felt it was not possible for her.

"Do you realize that's the third time in the past five minutes that you have said 'Stephen said'?"

Christy smiled mischievously at her young friend.

"For someone who is 'not in love,' you sure do talk about him a lot."

Esther looked down at her cup of coffee. The two women had had a wonderful evening of watching movies, eating, and chatting. Even though Christy was 30 years Esther's senior, she displayed a young heart. Yet, there were times Esther could hear the voice of experience from her. She ached to confide in Christy, but it was hard to let go of her need for independence.

"Esther, is something wrong?"

Christy sounded anxious, as if she were afraid she had offended her guest.

"No, it's okay. I mean, I'm fine."

Suddenly Esther made up her mind and leaned forward.

"Can I tell you something?"

"Sure! What's on your mind?"

Esther could see she had Christy's full attention.

"Do you remember when we were at the hospital, you told me to let others help me?"

Christy smiled tenderly at her.

"Yes, I do."

Esther sat quietly for a minute, struggling with her tears. This was harder to admit than she had thought it would be. As a tear slid down her cheek, Christy took her hand and squeezed encouragingly.

"I'm afraid," she finally murmured.

She looked up at Christy and honestly admitted, "I'm afraid to love someone."

"Can you tell me why?"

Christy's gaze was tender and supportive.

Esther nodded and took a deep breath.

"I was very close to my grandmother, my mother's mother," she started. "Mamaw was the one who taught me how to crochet and how to make divinity."

Christy remembered Esther's grandmother, a gracious woman with a strong, vital faith. Her divinity and banana pudding were favorites at church fellowships.

Esther continued her story, "When I was sixteen, Mamaw became very ill with pneumonia. I stayed with her as much as my parents would allow and prayed for her with just about every waking breath."

She sat and stared into the fireplace, lost in her memories.

The young girl sat quietly by her grandmother, listening to the elderly lady's shallow breathing. Tears rolled down Esther's cheeks. At sixteen, this was her first exposure to death.

She had never felt so much anguish and discouragement. Ever since the family had heard the diagnosis of double pneumonia, Esther had prayed frantically for her grandmother to get well. Now it seemed that God had not even heard her prayers.

Mamaw was getting worse. Even Esther's inexperienced ear could recognize the ominous rattle in her grandmother's breathing.

The door opened quietly and Esther's mother came in and sat on the other side of the bed. She reached across and took Esther's hand.

"I know, honey. It's hard to see her like this."

Her mother had tears running down her face.

"Mom, why hasn't God healed Mamaw?"

"I don't know, Esther."

"Did I pray wrong? Are my prayers not good enough?"

Esther tried to not sound whiny, but she was discouraged and angry. She was very close to her grandmother. They shared a love for old books and crafts. Her grandmother had taught her how to crochet. Mamaw had even taught her how to make her famous banana pudding and divinity.

"No, honey, that's not it."

Esther could see her mother was struggling with her own grief as she tried to comfort her.

"Then, why?"

Esther's mother sighed.

"I really don't know, Esther."

She squeezed Esther's hand and then let go.

"You need to go get something to eat and rest a while. I'll stay with Mamaw."

Esther wiped the tears from her cheeks and reached for another tissue.

"Mamaw died that night, while Mom was sitting with her. I felt for a long time that my prayers were not good enough."

Christy slid her arm around Esther and hugged her.

"Sweetie, I think you know now that that is not true. It was just time for your sweet grandmother to go Home."

Esther nodded.

"I know that now, but that's how I felt as a sixteen-year-old girl who had just lost her grandmother."

Too agitated to sit still, Esther got up and went to pour another cup of coffee. She didn't really want it, but she needed something to do with her hands.

Christy patted the sofa, inviting Esther to sit back down.

"Tell me the rest," she encouraged. "There is more, isn't there?"

Esther sat back down and stared into her mug.

"My family was very close. You knew that already."

She took a deep breath.

"We shared a lot of holidays, Sundays, or even just fun days together."

Esther managed a small laugh.

"We celebrated everything with food; good grades in school – sundaes for dessert; graduation from high school and college – big celebratory dinner. I'm surprised I'm not the size of a blimp!"

"About a month after I graduated from college, Mom and Dad were on their way home from a friend's house. There was a bad storm that night, they really should not have been driving. But Mom and Dad wanted to go home, so they were driving in pouring rain."

Esther stopped and shivered, lost in her thoughts. Slowly she picked up the thread of her story. "They hydroplaned on the highway and crashed into a tree. Both were killed instantly."

By now she was sobbing so hard she could hardly get the words out.

"I loved them so much, and then they were gone!"

Christy wrapped her arms around her in a comforting hug and just held her, rocking slightly. She yearned to be able to say something to comfort Esther, but this was a hurt too deep for words.

Esther pulled back and wiped her tears with the back of her hand. Christy handed her some tissues so she could blow her nose, then pulled out a few to wipe her own tears.

"Just a few months ago I lost Paul too. It seems that whenever I love someone, I lose that person."

She looked at Christy with agony in her eyes.

"I want to love Stephen, but I'm afraid if I do, something bad will happen and I'll lose him too."

Christy sat silently for a few minutes, giving Esther time to calm down. Inwardly she prayed for wisdom to help her. Finally, she answered Esther's unspoken question.

"You're wondering if it is ever going to be safe for you to love someone," she spoke softly. When Esther nodded, she continued, "Esther, what will happen if you decide you can't love Stephen?"

Esther looked confused for a moment. "What do you mean?"

"What will happen to your relationship with Stephen?"

"We'll still be friends," Esther sounded unsure. "I think."

"Is Stephen content to just be friends indefinitely?"

Esther looked away. Christy pushed her a bit. "Esther, do you think Stephen will be content to only be friends?"

"Are you saying that I could lose him if I don't love him?" Esther demanded. "Why does it have to be a romantic relationship? We're good friends; that should be enough, shouldn't it?"

Christy waited quietly for Esther to think it through.

Esther stopped and bowed her head. When she looked up, her expression was hopeful.

"Christy, I . . I think I may already be in love with him."

"Do you think he returns that feeling?"

Esther smiled tenderly, thinking about all the thoughtful things Stephen did for her.

"Yes," she nodded. "I think he does." Then she stopped as a frightening thought came to her.

"But, Christy, I'm afraid something bad will happen to him."

"You think loving someone makes something bad happen to that person? Wow! That's a powerful ability you have. You can make someone die by loving them!"

Esther had the grace to look embarrassed.

"Well, when you put it that way," she admitted, "it does sound stupid."

Christy took her hand again and squeezed it.

"I'm sorry, sweetheart, that's not what I meant. I'm not calling you stupid at all. I just wanted you to see that you loving someone does not make that person die. Only God gets to decide when someone will die. Esther, don't miss God's best for you because of fear. God's will is for you to live in freedom. Remember the memory verse you shared with the children in Sunday School last week? 'God has not given us a spirit of fear, but of power …'"

"'And of love and of a sound mind.'"

Esther finished the verse. She felt like a huge load had just lifted off of her.

"Thanks, Christy. I appreciate you so much. You and David have always been such good friends. I think I'll go to bed now. I need to have a long talk with God about this fear I've been carrying around."

Christy hugged her and told her good night.

Esther sat in the rocking chair in the guest room and tried to organize her thoughts before praying. When she was talking to Christy, it seemed so easy to just give in and allow herself to love Stephen. But now, sitting in the silence alone, her fears came back to her.

"God, I don't know what to do here," she confessed. "I think I'm falling in love with Stephen and it scares me. We've been good friends for several months, sharing a lot of fun times. I am so attracted to him. He is smart, funny, kind, and godly. I love how those chocolate brown eyes twinkle at me."

Esther sat, lost in thought for a moment.

"Lord, is it okay to allow myself to love this man? Am I sinning by being fearful and anxious?"

She tried to be quiet and wait for the Lord's answer, but her desire to find out if she could have a romantic relationship with Stephen distracted her. Before she went to bed, she made the decision. She would try moving beyond friendship with Stephen.

Chapter 17

Stephen breathed in deeply, trying to calm his apprehension. He felt like he really needed to talk to someone about his feelings for Esther and their relationship. He knew Christy and Esther were having their girls' night tonight, which meant David would be banished either to the study or his workshop. Stephen hoped to find David in the workshop so that he could talk with him privately.

As he eased his car down the long driveway, Stephen was relieved to see the lights on in the workshop windows. He parked close to the workshop and quietly closed his car door. Ninja's massive head appeared in one of the windows and Stephen could see the German Shepherd was happily wagging his tail. With a quiet chuckle, Stephen knocked on the workshop door and, finding the door unlocked, stuck his head in.

"Hey, Stephen! Come on in."

David finished cutting a two by four and turned off his saw.

"This is a surprise. If you came to see Esther, you're in the wrong spot. She's with Christy in the living room."

"Actually, David, I came to see you."

Stephen looked at David hopefully.

"I really need some advice."

David laughed as he waved Stephen into the shop.

"I think I know the subject of that advice. Come on in and we'll talk. Would you like something to drink? I have coffee, water, and soft drinks."

Stephen gratefully accepted a cup of coffee and wrapped his large hands around the mug. Now that he was here, he didn't know where to start. Fortunately for him, David started the conversation.

"You're worried about Esther, aren't you?"

"Not so much worried about her as puzzled about where to go next."

As Stephen took a sip of the coffee, David eyed him quizzically.

"What do you mean?"

"You know that Esther and I have been friends since we met back in April."

David nodded. "Yeah, you told me about getting on her wrong side right off the bat."

Stephen winced, "She set me straight right off the bat too."

"I bet she did," David laughed. "But you two went out for coffee and found you have a common interest. You've been hanging out together since then."

"David, I'm in love with her, but all she wants is to be friends."

Stephen felt a huge relief as the words poured out of him. He had been struggling with his feelings for weeks.

"I haven't pushed it because, well, I don't feel worthy. I can't be her protector because she doesn't need a protector. Esther is highly skilled in multiple martial arts. When I first met her at our dojo, she had me on the mat in less than a minute."

David sat back in his chair, smiling.

"So, you feel you're not strong enough, is that it?"

"Yes!" Stephen jumped up. "That's it exactly! I know it sounds old-fashioned, but I feel I should be the one to protect her."

David thought for a minute.

"What would you say are your strengths?"

Stephen was puzzled.

"Where are you going with this?"

David nodded reassuringly.

"Just humor me. What do you think are your strengths?"

Stephen thought for a moment, seeking for the words that would answer the question without bragging or false modesty.

"I'm good at analyzing situations and then making a decision," he finally said. "I'm good at listening and really hearing what people are saying. I'm not as strong physically as I would like to be, but I am fairly agile. I'm a third-degree black belt in karate and jujitsu."

Stephen glanced over at Ninja and finished, "I'm good at throwing Frisbees and I grill a mean steak."

David laughed at the last part. "I wonder what Ninja would say about your Frisbee throwing," he chuckled.

Both men looked at Ninja, who simply swiveled his ears toward them, then lay his head down.

"Why did you ask me about my strengths?"

Stephen sat and turned to the older man.

"In the best relationships, Stephen, it's not a case of one necessarily having to be stronger than the other," David explained. "It's a matter of sharing your strengths. Remember in Ecclesiastes it says, 'Though one may be overpowered by another, two can withstand him.' When you and Esther faced that robber, she might have been overpowered if you had not stepped in when you did."

Stephen sat back, thoughtfully considering David's words.

"You're right," he admitted. "I hadn't thought about it that way. I just felt like I should have been the one to step in and save us both. But Esther's speed and skill confined him so that I could step in and disarm him."

Then he slumped down in his chair.

"But that doesn't solve the problem of how to get us past friends to something more. We're great pals, doing a lot of stuff together. But she doesn't seem at all interested in progressing to a romantic relationship. In fact, she has quite plainly told me that she is not interested in anything but friendship."

David stood up and clapped his hand on Stephen's shoulder.

"Don't give up," he encouraged. "I suspect she may be more interested than you think. I imagine you'll find she's just afraid of losing someone else right now."

Stephen stood up and shook David's hand.

"David, I really appreciate your taking time to talk with me tonight. I'll get out of your way now, unless you need help with something."

He eyed the pile of two by fours stacked by David's saw.

David followed his gaze to the wood waiting to be cut.

"Well, I could use your help with a playhouse," he replied hopefully. "I promised our granddaughters we would have a playhouse for them to use the next time they come over. The project has grown way bigger than I originally planned."

As Stephen followed David to the work area, he couldn't help feeling hopeful again. Maybe, with patience and persistence, he could win Esther's heart. He was definitely going to try.

The two men worked in companionable silence for a while. After sanding the last board for the playhouse, Stephen put down the sander and stretched. He refilled his coffee mug and watched David for a minute, considering what he wanted to ask.

"Okay, Stephen, you look like you want to ask me something."

David grinned as he set down his hammer.

"Out with it or it will bug you all night."

Stephen laughed. "You're right, I am curious about something."

He carefully set the mug on a coaster and turned to David.

"Do you know why Esther hates being grabbed?"

"Oh, yeah." David refilled his coffee and invited Stephen to sit. "There's a story there."

Stephen leaned closer. "I have as much time as you want to give me."

David sat thoughtfully for a moment, then looked up. "Esther has always been a petite, delicate-looking girl. When she was about ten years old a new kid started at her school. He was a little older than the others in their class and a lot bigger. His name was Jack Browning."

Stephen nodded to show he was listening. He was already getting an idea of what had happened, but he wanted to hear David's story to see if he was right.

"Jack delighted in bullying anyone who was smaller than he was. For some reason, he took special delight in tormenting Esther. Of course, he made sure there were no adults around when he did his bullying. He loved to hide and jump out at Esther, grabbing her and putting his face right in hers."

Stephen sat up, horror dawning on his face.

"Did he . . .?"

David shook his head.

"No, there was no sexual abuse, but he often left bruises and torn clothing. Esther didn't want to tell her parents or her brother because she feared if Jack got in trouble, he would hurt her even more the next time he got her. One day he grabbed her and demanded her purse. Esther loved her little purse because her grandmother had made it for her. There wasn't really much money in it, but Jack knew it was special to her, so he slapped her and tore it off her shoulder. After he ran away, Esther just stood there crying."

"Wait a minute," Stephen interrupted. "How do you know about all this?"

"Hold on, I'm getting to that part."

David took a long drink of his coffee while Stephen waited impatiently.

"I learned about it the day Jack took her purse. I was out on an errand and was driving home when I saw Esther standing on the sidewalk with her hands on her face, crying. I pulled over and went to see what was wrong. Christy and I have known Esther and Paul all their lives. They're almost like our own children. When Esther told me what that young man had done, I wanted to bust his, well, you know."

Stephen nodded. "I feel that way right now, too."

David continued, "I told Esther she needed to tell her parents, but she sobbed that she was afraid if she told them, Jack would hurt her more the next time. I was stumped. I could tell them myself, but Esther had a point. Jack was in her class and would be able to get even with her when there were no adults around."

"I sent up a quick prayer as I tried to comfort her. Then, a great idea came to me; it had to be divine inspiration.

A friend of mine had just opened a new karate school in Forrestville. He was accepting new students of all ages. I suggested to Esther that she ask her parents to allow her to enroll. You should have seen her face light up! Well, the rest you can figure out. She enrolled and has studied there ever since."

Stephen couldn't wait to ask, "Did the bully bother her again?"

David grinned. "Esther joined an after-school program to stay out of his way until she learned some self-defense. Several months later Jack tried again to grab Esther. She tried out the hold her sensei had shown her and had that bully on his knees begging to be let go. Esther said she made him promise to never bully anyone else. She threatened to find him and put him in that hold again if he broke his promise."

Stephen laughed. "I love it! Now I understand both why she hates to be grabbed and why she took up martial arts. Thanks for sharing that with me."

David nodded, his blue eyes twinkling. "You're welcome. It always helps to understand something else about the special women in our lives."

Chapter 18

Esther brushed her hair and checked her appearance in the mirror again.

"Ugh!" she thought. "I'm as bad as a teenage girl going on her first date."

Even though she and Stephen had gone out together for the past few months, tonight was different. Tonight, they were going on an actual date. And Esther had a bad case of butterflies in her stomach.

Esther had only been back in her house one day when Stephen called and formally asked her out to dinner. Since her decision to test the waters of a romantic relationship, Esther had been wondering how to move forward. His invitation to dinner following on the heels of her decision came as a pleasant surprise.

She looked in the mirror one more time. After trying and discarding at least a dozen outfits, she had settled on black dress slacks with a lightweight amethyst sweater. Her jewelry was simple and elegant; a small gold cross on a fine chain, and a gold and amethyst bracelet. Her hair was pulled back with gold barrettes which set off the delicate gold hoops in her ears. Esther nodded at her appearance and exited the bathroom, snapping off the light on the way out.

The doorbell rang as Esther entered the living room. She wiped her hands on her black dress slacks. She looked down at Ninja, who was standing by the door wagging his tail.

"I don't know what I'm so nervous about," she told him. "This is Stephen – my pal, my comrade, my buddy."

Esther sighed.

"And a very attractive man who has asked me out for dinner."

Ninja just cocked his head and looked up at her, laughing.

Stephen fidgeted on the front porch and resisted the urge to ring the doorbell again. He held a large bouquet of mixed flowers gently in his left hand while his right hand smoothed his hair back – again.

He was thrilled that Esther had agreed to go out on a date with him. He was also terrified. What if they didn't hit it off romantically and he had just ruined a great friendship? He knew he would always be her friend, but it would be awkward, to say the least.

He straightened up as the door opened and then his jaw dropped. Esther's creamy skin and silky dark brown hair were beautifully complemented by the rich jewel tones of the sweater. Her brown eyes sparkled as he gazed at her.

"Wow!" he exclaimed. "You look gorgeous!"

When she blushed and looked down, he reminded himself to tone down his reaction. Stephen didn't want to come across too strongly and scare Esther away. Ninja crowded in between them right then, so he reached down to rub Ninja's head.

Stephen's words were just what Esther needed to hear. She opened the door further and motioned him inside as she looked at him admiringly. The dark blue suit coat and gray slacks fitted him perfectly. Although his hair looked somewhat unkempt, probably because he had been running his hand through it, to Esther he was the most handsome man she had ever seen.

As Stephen stepped inside, he handed Esther the flowers.

"Oh, Stephen, they're beautiful!"

Esther buried her nose in a carnation and inhaled the spicy scent. Through the sweet aroma of the flowers she could smell Stephen's shampoo and cologne. Somehow, the two combined to make a special scent that was uniquely his.

Esther put the flowers in water, then went to grab her jacket and purse out of her bedroom. She knew Ninja was doing a lot better about being alone, but was still concerned about leaving him as she stroked his back and reminded him to be good. When she glanced up at Stephen, he nodded at her encouragingly, as if he knew about her misgivings.

Stephen walked out with her, pulling the door closed and making sure it was locked. Then he took her hand, laid it on his arm, and led her to his car. He opened his car door and helped her into the seat. Esther enjoyed his gentle courtesies. It was nice to be treated like a princess, she decided.

About twenty minutes later, they pulled up at a small restaurant cozily situated in a grove of tall pines. After opening her car door and helping her out, Stephen kept her hand in his as they walked into the restaurant.

Esther admired the cedar and wood building with its large picture windows and deep porch. Rocking chairs were lined up across the front, as if waiting for a passer-by to stop and rest a while. Autumn flowers cascaded from planters settled deep inside wooden barrels.

It was as cozy inside as it was outside. Small tables were scattered throughout a large room. In the back were booths and off to the right Esther could see a large party room where a family was celebrating a birthday. The squeals from the birthday girl as she opened her presents brought a grin to Stephen and Esther's faces.

A smiling hostess approached and Stephen gave his name. She escorted them to a small table covered with a snowy white tablecloth.

The table held lavender-colored candles and a delicate vase cradling a fragrant bouquet of amethyst and white carnations interspersed with lilies and greenery. Esther gasped in pleasure. Stephen had arranged the table setting in her favorite colors. She looked up into his tender gaze as he held her chair out for her.

"Stephen, this is so beautiful!" Esther exclaimed. "I don't know what to say."

Stephen covered her hand with his.

"You don't have to say anything," he replied. "Just enjoy it."

An apron-clad waitress arrived to take their drink orders and give them large glossy menus. Stephen ordered an iced tea while Esther decided she would like to try the cherry limeade. After the server left, Stephen and Esther perused the menus.

"It all looks so good," Esther told Stephen. "What do you like best?"

"Actually, this is my first time here," Stephen confessed. "I heard about it from a friend and decided it sounded perfect for tonight. I made the reservations and arrangements for the table setting by phone."

They studied the menus for a few more minutes, then decided the grilled catfish and shrimp sounded good. After the waitress brought their drinks and took their orders, Esther allowed herself a more leisurely view of the room.

Large paintings of landscapes and seascapes adorned the walls. The front of the restaurant contained a small store with old-fashioned crafts and candies. Esther planned to explore the bins before they left.

Stephen saw the object of her interest.

"Would you like to look around the little store while you wait for your food?" he offered. "We'll be able to see the table from there."

Esther considered for a moment, looking longingly at the sale bins, then smiled.

"No, we'll wait until after dinner," she decided. "Let's just sit here and talk. Tell me about your day. How did your classes go?"

Stephen launched into a story about one of his students acing a difficult history exam that he had given them that day.

"This kid could be teaching my class in a couple of years!" he joked.

Esther then told about her fourth-grade class deciding they wanted to have a petting zoo for the town's Fall Festival. Several of the children lived on farms and felt they could take care of the animals. One of the local farmers had already offered a calf and several lambs. The class had even decided to bring the rabbit they were caring for in the classroom.

"I'm not sure how it happened," Esther laughed, "but I'm now in charge of the petting zoo."

When Stephen laughed, Esther chuckled as she regarded him with amusement.

"By the way," she chortled, "I volunteered you as well. I didn't think you'd mind."

Stephen was just taking a sip of his tea and almost choked. He sputtered and gasped for a moment before he could answer.

"Me?" he objected. "I don't know anything about farm animals."

"That's okay," Esther reassured him. "Neither do I, but several of the children do. Also, their parents will probably help out. I hope," she added doubtfully.

Stephen watched her for a minute and then burst out laughing. Esther joined him and they were still laughing when their food arrived.

Esther drew in a deep breath and let it out in a contented sigh. The evening had been perfect. She and Stephen had lingered over their dinner, talking and laughing. She felt she could definitely get used to Stephen's thoughtful gestures, like the flowers and holding the door or her chair for her.

Now they were strolling hand in hand down Main Street in Forrestville. Stephen stopped at The Sweet Shop.

"How about some turtle fudge for dessert?"

Stephen knew Esther had a particular weakness for fudge, especially turtle fudge.

"I don't know if I have room for it."

Esther considered for moment, then grinned back at him.

"Let's get a large piece and split it."

As they entered the candy shop, Stephen felt a prickle at the back of his neck, like someone was watching them. He turned around just in time to see Kenneth Owens standing behind a delivery van across the street. A sense of unease slithered down Stephen's back.

"What's wrong?" Esther looked up at him with concern.

"I saw Ken Owens across the street," he replied. "He was watching you."

"It is a small town," Esther reminded him.

She slid her hand through his arm.

"Let's forget about Mr. Owens tonight. I'm having too much of a good time to worry about him."

Stephen understood what she was saying. In a small burg like Forrestville, one tended to see the same people over and over. He glanced across the street again as he followed Esther inside. Ken Owens met his gaze and held it for a long minute. Finally, he gave a short nod and turned back to the delivery van, leaving Stephen with a vague, uneasy feeling.

"I had a wonderful time tonight,"

Esther gently squeezed Stephen's hand as they meandered through the well-lit park. Stephen had parked down near the picnic tables so they could have a leisurely walk up Main Street and back. They were almost to the car now and Esther hated to see the evening end.

"The evening isn't over yet."

Stephen pulled her around to face him and smiled down at her as he tucked a strand of hair behind her ear. He cupped her cheek in his hand. Slowly he put his other hand around Esther's small waist and drew her close to him. She gazed up at him wordlessly.

Stephen bent and tenderly claimed her lips, kissing her like she was the most precious gift in the world. Esther clung to him and returned his embrace. When they drew apart, she reached up to caress his jaw. Then she laid her head on his shoulder, his arms gently cradling her.

They stayed like that for several minutes, then Stephen reluctantly ended the embrace.

"Are you ready to head home?" he asked Esther.

"Not really," she laughed. "But I guess it's getting late. I need to get back to check on Ninja."

They ambled back to Stephen's car, content to walk in companionable silence. Stephen opened the passenger door and Esther sank into the seat with relief.

"I loved the walk," she said, "I'm glad to be sitting now. My feet hurt."

Stephen laughed and started the car.

"Yeah, we walked quite a bit tonight," he agreed. Then he picked up her hand and brushed his lips over her fingers.

"I enjoyed every minute of it since I got to spend that time with you."

Esther blushed and looked down. When she looked up at him, her eyes were starry.

"I enjoyed it too," she admitted. "You sure know how to make a girl feel treasured."

Stephen was silent for the rest of the drive home. Esther wondered if she had said something wrong. She kept glancing at his profile, admiring his short, curly hair and wondering how it would feel to run her fingers through it.

When they got to her house, Stephen came around to open her door and pulled her into a long hug. He lifted Esther's chin and gazed into her eyes.

"Esther, I do treasure you. I want to always treat you like the rare jewel you are."

Esther reached up and feathered her hand through his hair, then laid it on his jaw. She was speechless at the wonder of being so cherished. Where this relationship would go was still a mystery to her, but she wanted to store up all the happy moments like this.

"Would you like some coffee before you go?" Esther asked Stephen.

"I'd love some," he replied, glad for a chance to extend the evening a little longer.

"If you want, I can let Ninja out while you fix it."

"That would be great."

Esther turned around in the kitchen and grabbed the coffee can from the cabinet.

"You guys go ahead out back and I'll join you as soon as I get it started."

"Come on, Ninja," Stephen called the big dog over. Ninja had been sitting and listening to them with his ears perked whenever he heard his name. Now he padded over and waited patiently for Stephen to unlock and open the back door.

"Be sure to turn on the back floodlight," Esther reminded Stephen.

When they stepped into the back yard, Ninja stiffened and lifted his nose in the air. Then he trotted over to the back fence. He stopped and growled at an object laying partly hidden in the grass.

"What's going on?" Esther had just stepped out on the back patio and noticed her dog's strange behavior. She looked curiously at Stephen.

"I don't know," he admitted. "Ninja just sniffed the air, then growled at something he found."

Esther hurried to where Ninja was standing, his posture stiff and alert. She noticed something white laying at his feet. She bent to look closer, then picked it up by one end., making sure to touch it as little as possible. The item was a new rawhide bone. When Esther turned the bone over and held it up to the light, she could see a sticky substance smeared all over the surface.

"Stephen, would you step in the kitchen and grab a gallon-size bag for me?"

Although surprised by her request, Stephen stepped inside to grab the bag.

"Here you go."

He looked closer at the bone.

"What's going on?"

Stephen could see that Esther was uneasy about something.

"I never buy this kind of chew toy for Ninja," she answered. "And look at this sticky stuff all over it. I've never seen something like that on a new bone, have you?"

Stephen felt a chill come over him. Someone had thrown the chew toy in Esther's back yard for Ninja to find. Was there something wrong with it?

"Esther, call Ninja and let's get inside," he urged. Stephen suddenly felt Esther and Ninja were too exposed out in the yard.

"Let's call Maggie and get her to test that bone."

Chapter 19

"Stephen, are you sure your parents won't mind us bringing Ninja with us?"

Esther fidgeted with her watch band as she glanced again into the back seat where Ninja lay. The big dog seemed a lot calmer than Esther was about meeting Stephen's family.

"Would you relax, please?" Stephen laughed. "They insisted that we bring Ninja too. They want to meet both of you."

He looked over at her tenderly.

"I have no doubt that my family will love you."

Just then Ninja let out a low woof. Stephen glanced in the rearview mirror and chuckled at the big dog.

"I know they'll love you, big guy."

Esther smiled back at him, then pulled the visor down to check her hair in the mirror. Stephen just smiled and shook his head.

"What did Maggie find out about the bone?" Stephen asked her, trying to distract her.

"She called me this morning and told me it looks like someone smeared syrup mixed with rat poison on the bone and threw it in the yard for Ninja. There were no prints, but she's still looking into it."

Esther shuddered.

"If Ninja had not been taught to leave anything strange like that, he could have died a horrible death."

Stephen nodded. "I thought about that too. I'm glad he's too smart to fall for a trick like that."

He clenched his teeth as he remembered how absorbed in each other he and Esther had been while walking downtown and in the park. They would have been easy targets.

Stephen determined to be more aware of their surroundings. Even as he courted Esther, he had to remember the possible danger surrounding her.

Stephen hit the turn signal and turned into his parents' long driveway. Out of the corner of his eye he saw Esther take a deep breath and wipe her hands on her jeans. It was time to for her to meet his family.

"They're here!"

Stephen and Esther heard the shouts when they pulled into the driveway of his parents' house, an old-fashioned wood frame with a large front porch. Ninja sat up and looked around, his ears perked up.

A pretty teenage girl with short curly brown hair met them as Stephen opened his car door. She grabbed Stephen in a fierce hug. He hugged her, then set her back from him a little.

"Hey, sis! Let me breathe, okay?"

"I'm so glad you're here!" she gushed. Then she saw Esther and Ninja and waved at them enthusiastically.

"Stephen, what are you waiting for?" she reprimanded her brother.

"Go open the door for your girlfriend and her dog so we can start getting to know them."

Stephen mussed her hair as he let go of her and went around to open Esther's door. Esther stepped out and opened the back door for Ninja. He jumped out and went around to meet the girl who was standing back watching. The shepherd approached her slowly and sniffed the hand she held out to him.

"Is that Ninja? Can I pet him?" she asked hesitantly.

Stephen took Esther's hand and led her over to the girl.

"Esther, this little squirt is my sister, Cyndy."

He laughingly stepped away as his sister tried to elbow him.

"Cyndy, this is Esther. It looks like you've already met Ninja."

Esther smiled warmly at the girl who was still standing with her hand extended to Ninja. He had decided he liked her and given her hand an approving lick.

"It's nice to meet you, Cyndy. I think Ninja is glad to meet you too. You can most certainly pet him."

Esther paused a moment.

"I should warn you though, once you pet him, he will follow you around wanting more."

Cyndy squealed with glee and started rubbing Ninja's head and back. He stood and wagged his tail at the attention.

The front door opened and an older woman came down the steps to greet them. Her softly graying hair was styled in a short bob that set off her chocolate brown eyes. When she smiled at the small group in front of her, her eyes lit up with love.

"Mom!"

Stephen wrapped his arms around her and hugged her tight.

"Mom, this is Esther."

Stephen turned to Esther and pulled her close to him. "Esther, this lovely lady is my mother, Shirley Abrams."

He looked up and saw his father coming down the stairs behind his wife. In contrast to her dark brown eyes and blond hair, Mr. Abrams' eyes were a startling blue and his hair was brown with strands of silver just beginning to show.

"And this handsome gentleman following after her is my father, Dean Abrams."

Stephen grinned slyly. "I've heard it said that good looks run in the family."

"Yeah, poor guy, they missed you."

Two young men stood behind Stephen's parents. Both had dark brown hair and brown eyes, but where one was tall and slender, the other was short and stocky.

"These two comedians are my brothers, Lee and Ray."

"Esther, we are so glad to finally get to meet you. Stephen has told us so much about you."

Shirley Abrams turned to Esther with a smile that was warm and gracious.

"Thank you, he's told me a lot about you as well."

Esther was already feeling at home with Stephen's family as she and Stephen followed his parents into the house. Esther motioned for Ninja to walk beside her. He left Cyndy and went to walk beside Esther. Cyndy followed the group as they entered the front hall.

Dinner was relaxed and the stories flowed as Stephen and his siblings reminisced about practical jokes they had played on each other. Ray and Lee laughed uproariously as they recounted the numerous times they had pranked Stephen.

When Esther expressed sympathy, his mother laughed.

"Stephen wasn't always the victim. I can think of a few times he pulled a prank on his siblings."

The brothers snickered as Stephen protested.

"When did I ever do a thing like that?"

He sat back in his chair with an angelic look on his face.

"Well, there was the sippy cup episode."

Stephen jumped up.

"I think I'll get another cup of coffee. Would you like to join me in the kitchen, Esther?"

"Oh, no," she replied, her brown eyes sparkling.

"I want to hear the whole story."

Stephen sank back into his chair and groaned.

Shirley grinned at her son as she leaned forward.

"I think Cyndy was about two years old at the time. I was busy folding clothes when she came in and asked for a cup of milk. I should have been suspicious when Stephen volunteered so quickly to get it for her, but I just thought he was being nice."

She shook her head. "I should have known better."

"Hey, I'm nice!" Stephen protested.

Shirley ignored him and continued her story.

"We still had Cyndy using sippy cups at that time. We had some that you could put either a sippy lid or a storage lid on. I heard Stephen in the kitchen getting the cup and the milk. Then there was silence for a minute. When I heard Cyndy fussing, I went into the kitchen to see what was wrong. Stephen had given her a cup with a storage lid. Cyndy couldn't figure out how to drink from it."

Esther elbowed Stephen.

"Ow!"

He rubbed the spot in his side where her elbow had connected with his ribs.

"That was a mean thing to do to your little sister!"

"It was fourteen years ago!"

"It still wasn't very nice."

Ray came to his rescue.

"Esther, do you have any prank stories to tell? Something you did or that someone did to you?"

Esther thought for a minute, then a grin came over her face.

"Yes, there was the time my roommates tried to sign me up for a bikini mud wrestling contest."

"What? No way!"

The family all leaned forward to hear her story.

"I was in my senior year of college. We were taking a break after mid-term exams and my roommates decided we needed to go out to celebrate. They told me we were going to a bar and grill that had various acts on Friday nights. They said they signed me up to demonstrate some jujitsu moves. I thought that was cool, that I would just demonstrate some of the holds."

Esther stopped to take a drink of her iced tea.

"When we got to the restaurant, I saw the big mud pit and wondered what it was for."

She sighed as she looked around the table.

"Yes, I lived a very sheltered life."

They all laughed.

"Please, tell us the rest." Lee encouraged.

"My friend, Tammy, handed me a shopping bag and said they had brought what I would need for my act. They thought I would wait until I got back to the bathroom to take it out, but I was curious and pulled it out of the bag at the table."

Esther looked down as a deep blush covered her face. She could hardly get the next words out.

"It was a *very* tiny bikini. When I saw that, then looked at the mud pit, it all came together for me. They wanted me to put on that skimpy bathing suit and get in the mud pit to wrestle with other women also wearing skimpy bathing suits. I was so shocked and angry that they would do something like that, all I could do was glare at them for a minute. I think I scared them. Maybe they thought I was going to toss them in the pit. Instead, I pushed back my chair and stomped down the aisle to the exit."

Shirley shook her head.

"I certainly understand your anger. I'm surprised you can tell this as just a prank."

Esther smiled at her.

"Oh, it gets better," she said.

"On my way to the door, this guy stepped in my way. He had been watching and decided he would intervene. I could tell he had already had a few too many beers and thought he was 'the man.' But he made one big mistake. He tried to grab me."

Stephen grinned. He knew what happened to people when they tried to grab Esther.

"Before Mr. Studly knew what had hit him, I put him in an arm bar, then 'helped' him into the mud pit. When he came up for air, the wrestlers in the pit grabbed him and pulled him into their contest. I was still angry at my roommates, so I didn't hang around to watch. I marched out of that restaurant out to my car. Then I drove away and parked at a diner about a block away."

"Why did you stop at the diner?" Dean asked. "Why didn't you go back to your dorm?"

"I thought about it. But my roommates had ridden with me and I was their ride back. I didn't want them to have to walk back to the college in the dark. I just wanted to make them *think* they were going to have to walk back or get a taxi. Our taxi service in that little college town was notoriously slow. My friends found me about thirty minutes later. They meekly came into the diner and sat down across from me. Then, one by one, they apologized for putting me in that situation. I think they realized they had gone too far with the bikini. They knew I wouldn't wear something like that."

Esther grinned at her audience.

"I might have considered the wrestling, though."

Stephen laughed.

"It wouldn't have been a fair fight. Weren't you already a black belt in jujitsu by then?"

"Yeah, and your point is?"

Dean and Shirley shook their heads.

"You better watch out, son," Dean warned Stephen. "This one's not going to take any nonsense from you."

Esther grinned.

"He's already learned that – the hard way."

She stood up from the table and stretched.

"But that's a story for another day. Stephen, it's getting late. We better head back. I need my beauty sleep."

Stephen stood in front of Esther and rested his hand on her shoulder.

"You're already beautiful. But, you're right. It's time to go."

Shirley came around the table and hugged Esther.

"We're so glad to get to spend this time with you."

She pulled back to look into Esther's face.

"Please come back and see us again."

Esther returned her smile and promised she would try to come back very soon. Stephen hugged his father and shook hands with his brothers.

Dean winked at Stephen and nodded his head toward Esther.

"This one's a keeper, son," he told him. "Don't let her get away."

Stephen grinned at his father.

"I was thinking that very thing, Dad."

He let his eyes rest on Esther tenderly.

"She is definitely a keeper."

Chapter 20

Kenneth Owens drew in a deep breath and released it slowly. His gaze traveled to the top of the closet. He knew he had to go through that box. He just wasn't sure he could do it.

After Jimmy's suicide in prison, his father had received a manila envelope with the few items Jimmy had with him in his cell. Ken had thrown the envelope containing his son's last earthly goods into a box of mementos. He had then stored the box in the top of the closet in the guest room. Now he was going to take it down and try to sort through the memories.

Tears streamed down the grieving father's face as he slowly opened the cardboard box and began sifting through a lifetime of photographs and childish drawings. He smiled sadly at the picture that Jimmy had drawn of himself with his parents when he was five. Those were good days, he thought. Before Ken's wife and Jimmy's mother died from a hemorrhagic stroke when Jimmy was ten years old.

After her death Ken and Jimmy had grown even closer. Ken knew he had spoiled his son and had not provided the discipline Jimmy needed. The young widower had not been able to bring himself to marry again, so he had had to be both mother and father to the growing boy.

Ken dug a little deeper in the box and found Jimmy's high school yearbook. The boy had been so bright and curious in school, always asking "why?" Then, his last two years in high school that attitude had changed to apathy and defiance. Jimmy had met other students with that same tendency toward rebellion and their bad attitudes seemed to feed off of each other. Ken felt that that was when he truly began to lose his son.

He found Jimmy's high school diploma and shook his head sadly. Jimmy had barely managed to finish high school. After graduation the boy had shown no inclination to go to college or get a job. He just hung around with his friends, shooting pool and getting drunk. He even came home high a few times.

When Ken demanded to know where he was getting the drugs, Jimmy just smirked and walked out without answering. Ken knew he should have put his foot down then.

"Should have, would have, could have," he muttered to himself.

He stood up to work out a crick in his back. When he turned back toward the box, his arm caught one of the flaps and knocked it over. The box tumbled off the bed and landed upside down on the floor.

Muttering curses to himself, Ken lifted the box off of the floor and knelt on the carpet to pick up the contents that were now scattered around the bed. He grabbed a sheaf of notebook paper and started to throw it in the box. A name on the top of the first page caught his eye and he pulled it closer to read it.

His eyes widened as he read, first the top page, then the others underneath. It was a list of drug transactions: who Jimmy got the drugs from, the quantity, how much he sold them for, how much he had to give to his supplier, and how much he kept for himself. Jimmy had not been a good student his last two years, but he had kept meticulous records of his drug trade. When the police chief's office had shown up at his door with a search warrant, they had given the box a cursory glance. Seeing it filled with childhood photographs must have convinced them that there was nothing there that they needed to see. Since these papers were in the bottom of the box, they had not been seen.

Ken groaned and dropped the papers on the bed. He could hardly bear to see it spelled out so clearly when for the past year he had accused Paul of unjustly arresting his son. Then an idea occurred to him. Snatching up the list, he perused it until he found what he was seeking – the name of his supplier. Jimmy had printed the name in the column with the amount he owed.

"Why am I not surprised?"

Ken had had his own suspicions about who was the head of the local drug ring. He knew the guy generally sent his dealers to sell in Shreveport and Longview, but some, like Jimmy, had tried to build a customer base in Forrestville. That was probably what had led to his downfall.

Now the question was, what was he to do with this information? Ken was reluctant to give it to the police chief. He knew she and her narcotics detective, Paul, had suspected him of being the supplier. Would they use this information against him? Would they arrest him or the guy whose name was on Jimmy's paperwork? He would just sit on this for a while. Besides, he wanted to deal personally with the man who had ruined Jimmy's life.

Chapter 21

The sounds of children laughing, music playing, and people talking all mingled in chaotic harmony as Esther struggled to get the baby lamb back in the pen. Every time she tried to close the gate the little fluff ball would stick his head in the way. Finally, Esther called out for help.

"Stephen! Could you hold this little guy until I get the pen secured? Then you can put him down inside."

Stephen carefully set down the cardboard carrier that was precariously holding their drinks and corn dogs and stepped over to the petting zoo Esther had set up. They had several lambs, kids, and a calf donated by a local farmer. Esther's fourth-grade class had donated the use of the class bunny. Ninja just sat by Esther's folding chair and looked bored, as if he knew that he would still be the favorite when the children came by.

"Stephen, you can put him down now."

Esther smiled in amusement as she watched Stephen cuddling the youngest lamb. Stephen looked as if he could hold that lamb all night. Esther had to admit to herself that the little guy was adorable. She also couldn't help thinking that the big guy was pretty adorable himself.

She stepped over to Stephen and lightly kissed his lips.

"What was that for?"

Stephen used his free hand to wrap around Esther's waist so he could snitch another kiss.

"Just because."

Esther caressed the lamb's head as she stepped just out of Stephen's reach and winked at him.

"You looked so cute with that lamb in your arms."

Stephen laughed and nuzzled the little one.

"Can I help it if I'm a sucker for baby animals?"

As Esther finished her corn dog, she saw a few children approaching their petting zoo. Behind them she thought she got a glimpse of Kenneth Owens. Stephen was right. Mr. Owens seemed to always be around when she was in town and it was beginning to give Esther the creeps. She thought about asking Maggie to check him out.

"Chelly, come feel this soft baby lamb!" Annie called to her sister. Esther smiled at the girls as they oohed and ahhed over the animals. One of the fourth-graders was showing another child how to hold the rabbit. Esther nodded her approval for him. As the children and their parents crowded around the small enclosure holding the animals, Esther felt a sense of gratification that she was able to contribute to the town's Fall Festival.

"Esther, can you come . . ."

Stephen's eyes suddenly went wide in shock. A second later the sound of gunfire split the air. Children screamed and ran to their parents, who were frantically rounding them up and covering them with their bodies. The animals milled around in confusion. The fourth-grader who had been holding the bunny was kneeling on the ground with his parents, the rabbit dropped on the ground and freezing in place.

Esther watched in horror as Stephen fell on his knees grimacing in pain. A red spot showed on his left shoulder, spreading out in the t-shirt he was wearing.

"Oh, dear Lord," she heard herself praying. "Dear God, please, not again."

Ninja was standing with his ears forward, growling. Esther was afraid he would try to chase the shooter, so she called him to her side. Ninja reluctantly complied, but his ears and eyes remained alert and vigilant.

She reached Stephen and knelt beside him, watching the crowd around her for whoever had taken a shot into a crowd of children. Esther vacillated between terror and anger; terror that Stephen would die and anger that someone would do something this cold and calloused.

Police chief Maggie Jones arrived quickly at the scene, calling into her radio for back up and an ambulance. Esther watched as the police chief took in the chaos and Stephen's injury.

"Easy does it, Stephen. That's a nasty looking hole in your shoulder."

Stephen tried to get up to protect Esther, but his head was spinning. The police chief gently pushed him back down to sit on the ground.

"Hang in there, paramedics are on the way."

Maggie turned to Esther; whose face was a pasty white.

"Esther, I think you better sit with Stephen and keep him still. Are you injured anywhere?"

Esther numbly shook her head and sat next to Stephen. She grabbed a roll of paper towels she had brought for clean-up and tore off a wad of them to press on Stephen's wound. She just couldn't believe this was happening.

While she waited for the EMT's to arrive, Esther scanned the crowd, making sure no one else was hurt.

The children who had been gathered around the petting zoo were being hustled into waiting cars by their parents. Other Festival attendees were standing around talking and pointing. Police officers had scattered throughout the crowd, looking for the shooter.

Ken Owens approached Esther with a concerned look on his face. Ninja growled low in his throat and stood in front of Esther. He didn't bare his teeth, but his posture was one of vigilance and protection. Owens stopped a few feet short.

"Miss Daniels, are you all right?"

He looked down at his hands, fidgeting with his hat.

"Look, this may not be the right time or place, but I need to tell you something."

Esther eyed him warily as she kept pressure on Stephen's wound. When Stephen winced, she murmured an apology. She fought the tears as she tilted her head back to look up at Ken.

"Go ahead, Mr. Owens, but make it quick. My friend here needs to get to the hospital."

Kenneth Owens looked down at Esther and Stephen, his face mournful.

"You know when my son died, I was furious with your brother. I thought Paul had killed Jimmy by putting him in prison."

He took a deep breath and seemed to fight to control his voice.

"I've had a lot of time to think about it since I threatened your brother and since he died. I realized that the person I really hated was myself. I was the one who spoiled Jimmy so bad that he thought he could do whatever he wanted without consequences. If it's anybody's fault, it's mine. So, I just wanted to let you know, I don't hate your brother or you, or even that dog anymore. I'm sorry if I caused any grief for your family."

Esther stared into the man's eyes for a moment, then her look gentled.

"Thank you, Mr. Owens. I accept your apology. I'm sorry for your loss, sir."

Owens nodded, then cleared his throat.

"If you like, I can put the tables and pens away if you can get someone to come get the animals. I want to help any way I can."

It seemed like an eternity to Esther, but it was only a few minutes until EMT's arrived and took over Stephen's care. One paramedic gently bandaged the entry and exit holes the bullet had left, while another one took Stephen's blood pressure. They hooked him up to IV's and carefully transferred him to a gurney which they loaded into the back of the ambulance.

One of the paramedics turned her attention to Esther, who was feeling shaky and dizzy by this time.

"Ma'am, are you hurt?"

The young EMT gently led Esther to sit at the back of the ambulance.

"Let me just check you over, then you can ride with him to the hospital if you like."

Ninja regarded the stranger warily, but allowed her to minister to Esther, with him sitting nearby.

"I'm fine," Esther responded automatically. The paramedic had her way, though, and checked her over swiftly and gently for injuries.

"I'm okay, really," Esther insisted. "I'm just shook up, that's all."

"That's understandable, ma'am. Just go ahead and sit next to Mr. Abrams. We'll get you to the hospital in a jiffy."

David and Christy arrived just as the paramedic finished checking Esther. They enveloped her with hugs and asked if there was anything they could do.

"Please break down the petting zoo for me," Esther pleaded. "All the farm animals belong to Mr. Mitchell. The bunny is mine. Can you just take him home until I can come get him? Mr. Owens said he'll take care of the tables and pens. Oh, and can you bring Ninja to the hospital? You can drive my car."

Esther handed David her keys, all the while fighting the urge to break down and sob. She was so worried about Stephen. He had tried to tell her he would be okay, but he was pale and obviously in great pain.

"Sure, Esther, we'll take care of it," Christy reassured her. "We'll be praying for Stephen, and you too. We'll be at the hospital as soon as we get things cleaned up here."

Esther nodded and leaned over to frame Ninja's massive head with her hands.

"I'll see you in a little while, big guy. Please go with David and Christy."

Ninja whined and licked her face. Esther buried her face in his fur for a moment, finding comfort in the dog's warmth. Then she moved back and released him. She stepped up into the back of the ambulance, finally settling where she could see Stephen's face, but stay out of the paramedic's way. She glanced out the back window of the ambulance and saw Ninja sitting with David and Christy. Esther leaned her head back and silently prayed all the way to Forrestville General.

Chapter 22

Jesse sat on a large boulder and watched the scene below him. He felt a chill deep inside that had nothing to do with the cold night air.

He shook his head and huddled deeper into his jacket. He had never felt so frightened in all his life. When that bullet hit Stephen Abrams, Jesse knew who had fired it, even though he had not seen the shooter. He knew his boss was getting angrier and more impatient each day. He also knew Frank was getting desperate to kill Esther Daniels and her dog.

Jesse and his aunt had had a long talk about what he could do to get away from his boss. He didn't want her to get hurt; she didn't want him working for a drug dealer and a murderer. Finally, Jesse agreed to think about it and pray about it. Although he had been a believer since childhood, Jesse knew he had wandered far from the faith.

"God," he whispered. "I'm scared. Things are getting out of hand and I don't want to be mixed up in this anymore."

Jesse stopped to wipe the tears from his cheeks.

"I know I don't deserve Your forgiveness and Your help, but I sure need them both. Aunt Abigail says that's why it's called mercy."

He strained his eyes to see what was happening at the Fall Festival. Most of the crowd had dissipated; the holiday mood spoiled by the shooting. Jesse couldn't see where Frank had gone. He tilted his head back to look at the stars.

"What do I do, Lord? It all seems so hopeless and I'm scared. How can I get away from this man without Aunt Abigail getting hurt or killed?"

Jesse sat quietly for a long time, remembering a line from a sermon he'd heard recently. The pastor had talked about doing what is right and leaving the results to God. At the time, Jesse thought the pastor didn't know what he was talking about. Now he realized that that was the only way he could get out of this mess. When he stood up, he still felt uncertain about what to do, but he felt a peace that God would guide him.

"Whatever You say to do, God, that's what I'll do," he murmured. "I'll do what is right and leave the results up to You."

Esther sat staring sightlessly at the walls of the hospital chapel. She shuddered as the sights and sounds of the shooting ran on an endless loop through her head. How could this have happened again? Someone she loved was shot right in front of her.

Someone she loved . . . Reality crashed in on her. This was exactly what she had been afraid of. She had allowed herself to fall in love with Stephen and even imagine a future with him. But Stephen had been shot by an unknown assailant, just like Paul.

"I'm mad at You, right now, God."

Esther tilted her head back to look at the picture of Jesus with the children that hung on one of the chapel walls.

"I thought You gave me the okay to date Stephen and fall in love with him, but now he's lying in the hospital fighting for his life."

She paused and closed her eyes, then shook her head.

"No, that's not right. I didn't wait for Your answer, did I? I just charged ahead and did what I wanted without regard for what You wanted or for what was best for Stephen. Now he's paying the price."

Esther shuddered and looked around the chapel. Suddenly the dim, quiet room didn't seem so peaceful. It seemed dark and threatening. Was that bullet meant for her? Had Stephen sacrificed his life for her?

She heard the chapel door open and glanced over to see Christy walking in, Ninja trotting beside her. Hesitantly Esther stood and moved toward them. She knelt to put her arms around her dog, trying desperately to hide the shaking that had taken control of her body. Finally, she stood up and looked Christy in the face, waiting to hear news that could destroy her world.

"Stephen?"

It was all she could say.

"He's okay."

There were tears in Christy's eyes as she wrapped her arms around the younger woman in a comforting hug.

"The doctor said the bullet went through part of his shoulder. There's some damage to the shoulder, but not as bad as we first thought. He'll just need to take it easy for a while to let it heal."

Esther broke down sobbing and Christy held her for a few minutes. Eventually the sobbing stopped and Esther stepped back wiping her eyes and sniffling.

"Thanks, Christy," she murmured. "You're a good friend. I need to see Stephen now. Ninja, come."

Esther picked up her purse and slowly walked out of the chapel. She could feel Christy watching as she pushed through the door out in the corridor. She knew Christy and David were worried about her, but she felt Stephen was the one everybody should be thinking about.

Esther felt her resolve harden. It would not be easy, but she would do what she had to do to protect Stephen, even if it meant tearing her own heart in two.

Stephen was released from the hospital a week later. Esther picked him up from the hospital and drove him home.

Something was different, though. Even though Esther was attentive, she seemed distant from him. She was gracious and helpful, but the closeness they had enjoyed was gone.

When they arrived at his apartment, Esther helped him inside and then flitted around the apartment tidying and fixing things up for him.

"Esther, would you please come sit down and relax?"

Stephen watched Esther put down the pillow she was fluffing and come sit across from him. He wished she would sit beside him. He missed her warmth.

Since the shooting, Esther had hovered over him, making sure he had everything he wanted or needed. But she would not sit with him or even talk to him other than asking if he needed anything.

"Stephen?"

Esther's voice sounded different to him. Like she was determined about something he wasn't going to like.

"What's wrong, sweetheart?" he asked her. "Come sit here beside me."

Esther just shook her head and looked down, fidgeting with her hands. Now Stephen was becoming alarmed.

"Esther, what's wrong?"

Esther jumped up and began plumping pillows again. Stephen resisted the urge to tell her to sit down. Finally, she sat in front of him again and looked him in the eye.

"I don't think we should date anymore."

Esther watched him flinch as if she had struck him. She hated telling him this, but it was for his own good, she thought.

"In fact, I don't think we should see each other anymore."

Stephen reached out for her hand, but Esther evaded him.

"Why can't we see each other anymore?" he demanded. "Esther, look at me!"

Esther met his eyes briefly, then looked away. She kept her head down, struggling to not throw her arms around him and tell him she loved him and wanted to protect him.

"Stephen, you were shot because of me!" she finally choked out. "Everyone I love dies! I don't want you to die because of me."

Stephen felt a brief thrill that she said she loved him, but then the rest of her sentence registered.

"You think if we continue to date, if you allow yourself to love me, that I will die?" he asked her gently.

Esther jumped up and paced back and forth in front of him.

"It always happens that way," she insisted. "My grand-mother, my parents, my brother. Then you were shot while you were out with me."

She leaned against the back of the chair and let the tears come.

"Esther, come here."

Stephen leveraged himself off the couch and went to put his good arm around her. For a moment she stayed in his embrace, then firmly stepped back.

"Goodbye, Stephen. I think it's best this way."

Esther picked up her purse and started toward the door.

Stephen stepped in front of her and reached for her, turning her to face him and tilting her chin up so he could look in her eyes.

"Sweetheart, you can't run from love because of fear. You have to decide if you are going to live in fear and loneliness or if you will live in faith and love. Remember what you said Paul told you? 'Don't let fear keep you from experiencing God's best for you.'"

He watched as her beautiful eyes warmed with love for him briefly, then become cool and distant.

"Goodbye, Stephen."

Esther turned and walked out the door.

Chapter 23

"Jesse! Where you been, man?"

Frank caught up with Jesse as he walked up the driveway to their employer's home. Their boss had summoned them for a meeting at his home office.

"I've been looking for you all week."

Jesse just looked at Frank and then turned his eyes away. He'd thought he and Frank were good friends, but he felt nauseated whenever he remembered Frank firing into a crowd of children in a desperate attempt to kill Esther Daniels and her dog.

Suddenly Frank stopped short and grabbed Jesse's arm, pulling him to a halt.

"What is wrong with you?" he demanded. "You act like you don't want anything to do with me all of a sudden. You think you're too good for me?"

"You tried to shoot Esther Daniels at the Fall Festival, didn't you?"

"Yeah, what of it?"

Frank looked puzzled.

"You heard the boss. He said to kill her and that dog. So, what's your problem?"

"You fired into a group of kids, that's my problem!"

Jesse glared at his friend.

"Doesn't it bother you that you're trying to take someone's life? Doesn't it bother you that you could have hit a child with that bullet?"

Frank shrugged, his acne-pocked face indifferent.

"I do what I have to do," he replied. "If I don't do what the boss says, then I'm the one that could get killed. So, I follow orders and get paid to do it."

Frank jeered. "What's your problem? You think you're too good to do the dirty work?"

He poked Jesse in the chest.

"You know you've already been selling drugs to little kids. Some of them might die from the drugs. You ever think about that?"

Jesse turned pale. Just the thought of those children dying because he sold them drugs made him feel sick. Before he could reply they heard a voice on their radios. "Frank and Jesse, in my office – NOW!"

Even though he had not yelled, the two knew their employer was angry. He had just returned from a two-week business trip and they knew he had probably heard about the fiasco at the town's Fall Festival.

"Well," Frank swallowed hard. "You heard the man. Let's go."

Frank and Jesse felt the chill as soon as they entered the boss' office. His face was like granite and his eyes even colder than usual.

"Hi, boss!" Frank tried to be jovial. "How was your trip?"

His employer just looked through him, then curtly motioned for them to sit down. Frank sat in one of the chairs in front of the desk. Jesse chose a seat on the sofa near the door. He knew things were probably about to get ugly, and he wanted to be able to escape quickly.

"Tell me about the shooting at the Festival."

Frank looked down at his hands, then craned his neck to look back at Jesse.

"Look at me when I address you, Frank. Tell me about the shooting."

Frank took a deep breath.

"Well sir, I'm a pretty good shot, so I thought I could pick off the woman and the dog and then get away during the confusion afterward. Since there was a lot of yelling and people were crowding around, I was able to get away without anyone noticing me. I'm good at camouflage, so I don't think . . ."

"That's the problem, you don't think!"

The boss was standing now, leaning over the desk with his hands braced on its surface.

"You imbecile! You idiot! Four times you have tried to kill this woman and her dog and four times you have failed! You couldn't even complete the one simple assignment that I gave you."

He took a deep breath.

"It would seem if I want the job done right, I'll have to do it myself; which I will – today. And, *I'll* do it right!"

He sat down; his face stony.

"You disgust me. Get out of my sight!"

Frank stood and glared at the man with hot, angry eyes.

"I've done everything you said," he retorted hotly. "I've stolen for you, sold drugs for you, and killed for you."

He slammed his hands down on the desk. Jesse winced as he watched his coworker confront the man who employed them.

"You haven't killed for me," the boss sneered. "You missed – four times. You are ineffective and useless. Now get out of here!"

Frank suddenly let loose with a tirade of profanity aimed at the man behind the desk, then stormed out of the room, slamming the door behind him. He stomped to his little hatchback and peeled out of the driveway, heading toward downtown Forrestville.

The boss just sat there, sorting through papers stacked on the desk. Jesse slipped out of the room, hoping the boss wouldn't see him. After his experience with Frank and the scene he had just witnessed, Jesse knew what he had to do. He started his truck and turned it toward town, heading toward the police chief's office.

Chapter 24

Jesse hesitated as he drew near the police chief's office. He realized that Police Chief Jones might decide to put him in jail for dealing drugs and he knew he could not afford to go to jail. Because of her recent illness, Aunt Abigail needed him at home to take care of her. He sat in the truck trying to think. Jesse knew he needed to tell someone what was going on, especially if the boss was going to try himself to kill Esther and Ninja.

Stephen.

Jesse had heard through Aunt Abigail that Stephen was being discharged today. Esther would probably be at Stephen's apartment. He called his aunt.

"Aunt Abigail, do you know where Stephen lives?"

"Sure, honey, but why do you need to know?"

"I'll tell you later, but I really need that address now. I need to talk to him. It's really important."

"Hold on a minute, I have it right here."

Jesse scribbled the address on a scrap of paper. Just before hanging up, he asked his aunt to pray.

"You know I will," she assured him.

Jesse hung up and turned his truck toward Stephen's apartment complex. He hoped Stephen would listen to him and tell him what he could do.

After Frank and Jesse left his office, the boss sat at his desk trying to concentrate on his work. His demeanor of calm masked a raging spirit. Finally, he slammed his pen down on the desk.

"I am surrounded by fools!" he growled. "Absolute, ineffective, stupid, idiotic, fools!"

The big man got up and paced the length of his office. with a heavy tread.

"Jesse was a mistake. I never should have hired him. He doesn't have the guts to do what needs to be done. Always worrying about if it's right or wrong. Always worrying about what his aunt will think. He's nothing but a mama's boy!"

He stopped and stared out the window for a moment, then resumed his pacing.

"Frank is a big disappointment to me. I thought he was loyal and smart, but he couldn't even do the simple job I gave him. Messed up four times! Now the police chief will be suspicious. I can't afford to have any suspicion on me. Not after that fool kid, Jimmy Owens, got caught trying to deal in Forrestville. Idiot! I told them not to sell here! I'm glad he killed himself. Saved me the trouble."

The businessman sat down at his desk and leaned back in his comfortable leather chair. He thought about the money in his safe.

"I could just leave this all behind," he mused. "Just take the money and go somewhere far away. Somewhere that has no extradition agreement with the U.S."

He sat up straight.

"I'll take care of that woman and her dog myself. I"ll get done what Frank should have done. Then I'll leave this miserable little town and this miserable country as far behind as I can."

He picked up an expensive leather satchel and marched to the safe. As he opened it and began taking money out, he heard a hesitant tap on his door, then the sound of the door opening. His housekeeper's head poked in the door. Her eyes went wide as she saw him stuff the last stack of money into the satchel.

"What do you want?" he roared at her. "You know I told you that you're never to open that door unless I say so!"

The housekeeper started talking quickly, hoping to escape her employer's ire.

"I just wanted to know if you were going to be here for dinner."

"NO! I won't be here for dinner, breakfast, or anything else," he shouted. "Now get out of here! Scram!"

The housekeeper retreated to the kitchen where she recounted their conversation with the maid. The two of them could hear as their employer stormed up the stairs into his bedroom. He was muttering about leaving and about a woman and a dog.

The two women watched with astonishment as he stomped down the stairs. When he saw them staring at him, he growled at them.

"Get back to work! I don't pay you to stand around staring at me."

They took a deep breath of relief when he rushed out to his car and sped away.

"Some days I just don't understand that man," the housekeeper tsked.

"I don't understand him any day," the maid agreed. "In fact, he kind of scares me. I think I'm going to give notice and take a job in Shreveport. I saw a good one in the paper this morning."

"Do you think they'd want a housekeeper too?"

Ken Owens sat alone in a booth at Pot O' Gold. Since it was just before the bar's 5:00 Happy Hour, it was still fairly quiet. There were a few other patrons scattered around the tables and booths. One of them was a rail-thin young man with acne and a scraggly beard. Ken had watched idly as the young man finished one pitcher of beer and started on another.

Ken finished his drink and sat thinking as he idly swirled the ice in his glass. He had found evidence of his son's drug trade. That in itself was enough to send him reeling. But he also knew who had hired Jimmy and paid him to sell that poison to other kids.

As he stewed in his own morose thoughts, he heard muttering from the pimple-faced kid. Ken looked up and narrowed his eyes. He knew who the drunk was; had even hired him to do contract work for the hardware store at times.

Ken knew Frank worked for the city and now knew Frank had also sold drugs for the same man Jimmy had worked for. He wondered what had Frank so worked up now. He got up and walked over to Frank's table.

"Mind if I join you?"

Frank looked up and waved his hand.

"Whatever," he muttered.

"What's eating you?"

"My boss is an idiot! He's an imbecile! He's an ingrate!"

Frank was working himself up now.

"I worked my tail off doing whatever he told me to do. Now he tells me he's disgusted with me! Just because I couldn't kill, uh, finish something he wanted me to do!"

Ken Owens startled. Did the kid just start to say his boss wanted him to kill someone?

Frank jumped up from his chair.

"You know what?" he slurred. "I don't care anymore. I'm going home to crash and tomorrow I'm going to tell him what he can do with his job."

After Frank left, Ken sat and went over their brief conversation. Then he thought about the evidence in his closet. As he mulled it over, he made a decision. It was past time for something to be done about the jerk who was ruining other people's lives – and he was going to do something right now.

Esther drifted restlessly around her house. She could not get Stephen's words out of her mind.

At first, she was incredible angry that he used her brother's words to try to reach her. How dare he! Sharing that with Stephen had made her feel closer to him. But hearing those words come from his mouth as he tried to get her to not break up with him just rubbed her the wrong way.

She moved into her little kitchen and began fixing herself a cup of tea. Why did he have to remind her of what Paul had said? Esther felt the tears sting her eyes again. Was she wrong to break up with Stephen because she was trying to protect him?

Ninja trotted into the kitchen, his nails tapping on the hard floor, and sat by the back door. Esther smiled through her tears. She loved this dog. He always knew when she needed a distraction.

"Okay, boy, we'll go out in the backyard and I'll throw your ball for you a few dozen times."

Esther opened the door and followed her dog outside into the cool November air. Ninja found his old tennis ball and brought it to Esther to throw.

As Esther played with Ninja, she realized she had never really faced the fact that she was afraid to love. She had discussed it with Christy and knew it had affected all of her relational decisions. But she had never fully looked it in the face. Esther knew she was letting fear keep her from loving.

One of her favorite Bible verses came to her mind, "For God has not given us a spirit of fear."

Esther automatically threw the ball for Ninja while her mind was far away.

"God doesn't give me this kind of fear!" she said aloud. "He gives me a spirit of power and of love and of a sound mind."

Laughter bubbled up inside her.

"Why in the world have I done this to myself?" she marveled. "I don't have to live afraid of losing someone. I need to live with my heart and my life full of God's love."

Suddenly Esther felt free. When Ninja brought the ball back to her, she took it from him and told him, "We're going in now, boy. I need to call Stephen. I need to tell him he was right!"

She paused a moment in awe.

"I need to tell him I love him."

As Esther opened the back door and started in the house, Ninja started growling and snarling. Reflexively, Esther grabbed his collar until she knew what he was growling at. She didn't want him tangling with a snake or other creature that might have sneaked into the house to avoid the cold.

"Esther, my dear, you need to crate your dog so that I will not need to shoot him. At least, not yet."

Richard Grayson was in her house, pointing a gun at her and Ninja.

Chapter 25

Stephen stood staring at the door for a few minutes, almost expecting Esther to return to say she didn't mean it and that she wanted to stay with him.

Finally, he turned away and went to stand by the couch. Realizing he was too angry and restless to sit, he grabbed his phone and keys. The surgeon at the hospital had told him to take it easy for a few weeks, but Stephen reasoned that a walk wouldn't hurt him any. He needed to think and he needed to move.

At first, he almost jogged down the sidewalk, but the pain in his injured shoulder reminded him to slow down. Stephen walked slowly down the block. At the corner he debated continuing to the coffee shop, but the increasing pain made him decide against it. Stephen trudged through his apartment door, dropped his keys on the counter and eased into his chair; his shoulder painfully protesting the exercise.

Esther was really gone.

Stephen came out of his fog to realize that his doorbell was ringing. He considered not answering, but then hope sprang inside that Esther might have come back. He opened his door to find Jesse on his doorstep. He regarded his visitor warily.

"Can I help you?"

Stephen had only met the young man twice. He wondered why Jesse would even be at his apartment.

"Stephen Abrams?"

At Stephen's nod, Jesse rushed on.

"I know who shot you. And I know who hired him to do it."

"Jesse, before you go any further, I think you need to tell this to the police chief."

Jesse turned white.

"I'm scared to," he confessed. "I've done some things myself, and I'm afraid she'll put me in jail."

Stephen felt sorry for him. He knew Jesse was very close to his aunt and was worried about her frail health. If he went to jail, Abigail would be alone.

"Maggie's cool. She's the kind that will work with you. It's better if you go to her than it is if she has to come find you."

Jesse thought about that for a moment, then his shoulders slumped.

"Okay, but can you get her to come here?" he pleaded. "I want you here too."

"Why?"

Stephen was curious why this young guy, who hardly knew him, would want him nearby to hear what he had to say.

"I don't know. I just feel like you need to hear it too."

Stephen picked up his cell phone.

"I can go with that," he agreed.

When Stephen heard Maggie pick up her phone, he told her about Jesse's statement.

"The poor kid is scared to death you'll put him in jail. He thinks it will be easier if you will come here and let us both hear what he has to tell us."

Maggie hesitated.

"Stephen, we're about to make a major arrest. Is this something that can wait?"

Jesse heard her and raised his voice so she could hear him.

"Chief Jones, it might have something to do with your arrest. It will only take a few minutes. Please come."

Jesse had no idea who they were about to arrest, he just took a blind guess. He heard Maggie tell Stephen she would stop by on her way out.

"It will have to be quick and it will have to be good," she warned.

When Maggie arrived, Jesse shivered at the sight of her uniform, with the nightstick and gun strapped to her waist.

"Richard Grayson is a drug dealer," he blurted. "Frank Parker and I work for him selling cocaine. Grayson buys the dope and then gives it to us to sell in places like Shreveport and Longview."

Jesse stopped to take a deep breath.

"He's also the one who killed Paul Daniels. When he found out Esther was there the day of the killing and that Ninja survived, he ordered Frank to kill her and her dog."

Stephen moved as if to jump up, but Maggie grabbed his arm.

"Hold on," she commanded. "There's more, isn't there?"

Jesse nodded and continued, "I wasn't with them that day. Mr. Grayson doesn't trust me for the heavy stuff, yet."

He shook his head.

"I'm glad. I feel horrible enough about what I *have* done for him. Selling drugs to kids." He slumped in his chair.

"I feel like the lowest of the low."

"We're not really interested in your feelings right now, Jesse. Get on with your story. I have somewhere I need to be and you're holding me up."

Stephen had never heard Maggie sound so cold.

"I've only heard bits and pieces about that day, but I put it together. Mr. Grayson and Frank were supposed to meet a new supplier. They chose the Michaels' place because it's remote and the Michaels were supposed to be gone that weekend. I hung out around Mr. Grayson's estate doing odd jobs so I'd be ready when they got back. A few hours later Frank and Mr. Grayson got back and came in the house. Mr. Grayson was incredibly angry and his right arm was hurt. It looked like something had chewed on the sleeve and he was bleeding."

At this Stephen and Maggie exchanged a significant look. That matched up to what Stephen had heard from his friend.

"What else can you tell us, Jesse?" Maggie's voice was warm and gentle now, like she was coaxing the information from him.

"Mr. Grayson didn't want to have to answer any questions at a local doctor about how he got hurt, so he went to an ER in Longview and made up a story about teasing a friend's dog. After he got patched up, he told Frank and me to take the SUV and Frank's car to Mississippi and sell them. He said Frank could pay me for going with him, and then could keep the rest to buy another vehicle."

Jesse let out a snort. "Frank bought a sweet little hatchback in Arkansas, then turned it into a junk car in just a couple of months."

He stood up and started pacing. Stephen and Maggie kept quiet so he could continue.

"I actually enjoyed the few months that Mr. Grayson was gone. Frank and I sold off the cocaine that Mr. Grayson had bought. Then we just did our jobs for the town and laid low. I was already thinking about getting out when Mr. Grayson came back in September. He was all revved up about a new supplier he had connected with while he was gone."

Jesse paused and ran his hand through his hair.

"When I told him I didn't want to work for him anymore, he just smiled that evil smile of his and said I could leave any time I wanted. Then he added that he just hoped nothing bad would happen to my aunt."

He turned tortured eyes to the two watching him.

"I couldn't let him hurt my aunt, could I? He knew he had me right then."

Nervously he fidgeted with his keys.

"I kept working for him, but I hated every minute. I think he wanted Frank to show me how to tamper with Esther's heater, but that was the same day that Aunt Abigail had to go to the hospital with pneumonia, so instead I wound up going to the hospital. The next day, when I went to visit my aunt, I saw Esther coming out of the hospital. She was so nice to me, asking me about Aunt Abigail. All I could think of was that I knew who almost killed her!"

Stephen leaned forward.

"What about the truck rolling and the shooting?"

"Frank just lucked out with the truck rolling. He was downtown the same day you and Esther were at the park. He saw that old truck sitting there, right at the place before the road slopes. It didn't take much for Frank to release the brake and just sort of, you know, lean on the back bumper."

"The shooting was an act of desperation. He actually had tried to plan a shooting before that. He dressed all in black and tried to rob you and her. He was actually planning to shoot her anyway, even if she cooperated, and ditch the jewelry."

Jesse laughed.

"Esther scared the daylights out of him when she turned the gun around on him and then kicked the knife out of his hand. Boy, he sure hated telling Mr. Grayson about that. After Esther survived the robbery, the rolling truck and the gassing, Mr. Grayson told Frank to 'Just kill the woman and the dog. I don't care how!' Frank's a fairly good shot, so he thought he could just take advantage of the crowds at the Fall Festival and take out both of them before anyone noticed. He wasn't counting on someone getting in the way."

He glanced at the bandage and sling on Stephen's shoulder.

"He wasn't counting on you getting in the way."

Jesse sat up in his chair and stared into space, lost in thought for a moment.

"Mr. Grayson doesn't get loud when he gets mad. He gets cold and his voice has this bite to it. He told Frank to get out of his sight. I took advantage of Frank leaving and snuck out too. Then I came here. I can't let him hurt anyone else."

He looked pleadingly at the police chief.

"You won't let him hurt Aunt Abigail, will you?"

Stephen glanced at Maggie and was surprised to see a look of satisfaction on her face. She looked as if she had had something confirmed that she already knew.

Maggie laid a comforting hand on Jesse's shoulder.

"You did the right thing coming to us, Jesse. Don't worry, we're not going to let Mr. Grayson or Frank hurt anyone else. Go on home and stay with your aunt for a while now, okay? I'm not going to arrest you right now, because I have bigger fish to fry. But I need you to stay available."

Jesse blew out a relieved breath and stood up.

"Yes, ma'am. Thank you."

"Can you use his testimony?" Stephen asked her. "Is that your big arrest today?"

Maggie smiled a tight, secretive smile.

"His testimony will help," she commented briefly. "I've also got some other evidence. You're not the only one who's been keeping eyes and ears open."

As Maggie stepped out the door, she got a call on her radio.

"Hey boss, we went to serve warrants on Grayson's house and office. He's not at either one."

Jesse looked up; his eyes wide.

"Chief Jones, Mr. Grayson said he was going to take care of killing Esther and Ninja himself. He could be at her house right now!"

Maggie nodded.

"Meet me at Esther Daniels' house," she radioed her police officer. She gave the address as she dashed to her car.

Stephen waited just until Maggie pulled away, then turned to Jesse.

"Do you want to help me?" he asked the frightened young man. "I need to get to Esther's home before that madman kills her."

"What will you do?" Jesse asked. "Mr. Grayson probably has a gun with him and he's determined to kill her."

"I don't know," Stephen answered grimly, "but I'll figure it out when we get there."

Jesse motioned to his truck.

"I'll drive."

Chapter 26

"Mr. Grayson, how did you get in my house? Why are you pointing that gun at me?"

Esther was startled to see the businessman in her home. The man who had always seemed gentle and kind now had a hard, cold look in his eyes. His hair was standing on end, as if he had been running his hand through it and pulling on it. His suit was rumpled and his tie crooked. Esther could not believe the difference in the man.

"Never mind the how and why, my dear. We will talk about that after you put your dog in his crate."

Although he sounded controlled, Esther could see a wild, desperate look in his eyes. He seemed like he was barely keeping himself together. She knew she should be grateful that he did not just shoot the both of them on sight.

Ninja fought going into the crate, but Esther commanded him sharply. She did not doubt for a minute that Grayson would shoot him at the least sign of resistance. Finally, she got the angry dog in the crate and secured the latch.

"Very good. Now move over here away from him."

Grayson kept the pistol pointed at Esther as she stepped carefully away.

"Mr. Grayson, I don't understand. What's going on?"

"I'm afraid your dog does not like me at all. Probably because I'm the one who killed his partner."

Grayson replied as graciously as if they were having tea instead of discussing the murder of her brother.

"You killed Paul? Why?"

Esther was still having trouble taking it in.

"Yes, and I thought my associate had killed the dog. You see, they interrupted a, ah, business meeting I was having. When that dog," Grayson spat the words out venomously, "alerted on the trunk of my employee, I knew I would have to kill them."

Esther was stunned. She could not absorb the news that this respected, genial businessman was selling drugs and had murdered her brother. She realized that he had nothing to lose by killing her and Ninja. The fear clawed up her throat until she remembered what she had learned just a few moments before.

"Lord," she prayed. "Please give me that power and peace now."

As Grayson paced her living room and ranted on about how Paul had ruined everything, Esther began to plan how to take him down. She knew she would need Ninja's help, so she looked for ways she could release him while her enemy was occupied. She needed to move the man out into an open area so that she would have room to fight him.

Grayson adjusted his tie and cleared his throat as if preparing to give a speech.

"You know I have a certain reputation in Forrestville. If the townspeople knew my other source of income, well, they might not understand."

Esther remembered David talking about finding the white powder on the picnic tables at the murder scene and looked at the businessman with contempt.

"Your 'other source of income' is the sale of cocaine," she bit out. "Your 'other source of income' kills young people and destroys lives."

"Ah, yes, that's the mindset I was trying to avoid. That's why I always had my people sell the drugs in another area. Never in Forrestville."

Grayson waved the gun at her.

"But that has all been ruined now. I didn't know you saw the murder until the evening I talked with you after I got back in town. That's also when I learned that the dog had survived."

Esther realized that Grayson probably did not have a plan when he broke into her house. If he had been thinking straight, he would have just shot Ninja, then her, when she came in the house. While Esther was thankful for that slip on his part, she knew she needed to move quickly before he came up with a way to eliminate her and her dog.

"I was still in the woods when you murdered my brother," Esther informed him. "I didn't actually see it happen."

As she spoke, Esther took a small step in the direction of Ninja's crate. She glanced at Grayson to see if he had noticed, but he was pacing the length of her living room. One hand still held the gun while the other waved in the air as he ranted on. Esther took a few more steps, then stopped before he turned around. Grayson continued as if he did not hear her. He paused and pulled out a handkerchief to mop his forehead.

"I had to get rid of you two before you decided to tell what you saw. My helpers turned out to be stupid, incompetent fools who could not complete a simple assignment like killing a woman and a dog."

"You were behind the attempts on my life?"

Esther was beginning to understand. The attempts on her life had begun after her talk with Grayson, when she had told him she was with Paul that day.

"They were ineffectual attempts," he said. "But you know the saying, 'If you want something done right, you have to do it yourself.'"

As Grayson turned to pace the other direction, Esther slid a little closer to Ninja's crate.

"If you kill me and Ninja, people will know you were here. Some of my neighbors probably saw you enter the house."

Grayson shook his head as he continued his frenzied pace across her living room.

"It doesn't matter," he finally muttered. "I'm leaving this hick town anyway and starting fresh a long way from here."

Esther carefully sidled the rest of the way to the crate and unlocked it while Grayson's back was turned. Before Ninja could come out, she motioned to him to stay and whispered, "stealth and guard."

The K9 gazed at her steadily, then lay down, his eyes trained on Esther.

Grayson stomped over to Esther and glared at her, his eyes red and angry.

"What are you doing? Get away from there. This whole mess is all your fault!" he roared.

Esther stood and moved into Grayson's space. Instinctively he moved back, just as Esther had hoped he would. She needed him away from the furniture in her small living room.

"Wait a minute," she protested as she continued to back him into open space. "*You* decide to sell illegal drugs, *you* commit murder and attempted murder, and this is *my* fault? What kind of stupid reasoning is that?"

Esther knew that last part would enrage him. She wanted to distract him from seeing Ninja as he crept out of his crate and out of sight.

Grayson grabbed Esther's arm. Instinctively she pivoted around to grab his hand and point the gun away from herself. When she took hold of his wrist, he tried to use the other hand to strike her on the side of the head. Esther held on and ducked, pushing him away as she grappled for the gun. The pistol fell and bounced under the coffee table. Grayson stepped back to try to keep his balance.

With a ferocious snarl, Ninja launched toward the big man and latched onto the same arm he had bitten when Grayson killed Paul.

Screaming curses, the man raised his other fist and deliberately slammed it into Ninja's injured shoulder. Ninja yelped in pain and dropped to the floor.

When she saw the vicious attack on her dog, Esther went white-hot with anger. She moved with swift precision as she approached the killer and began striking and kicking. Grayson tried to back away, helpless against her onslaught. Finally, she swiped her leg beneath his ankles, knocking the big man to the floor. He fell hard, striking his head, then lay still for a moment.

Breathing hard, Esther started toward where the gun had fallen.

Grayson groaned and looked over at the gun as well. He struggled to his knees to get to the pistol. Just as his hand reached for the weapon, he felt a cold nose in the back of his neck.

The drug lord turned to see an angry, snarling German Shepherd right behind him. He shrieked and fell over with Ninja looming over him, lips drawn back and fangs gleaming.

Esther picked up the gun carefully and unloaded it, checking the chamber as well. Then she pocketed the weapon and turned to her assailant.

"If you lay very still, maybe he will not attack you," she told the quivering man on her floor. She decided to make a point.

"However, Ninja knows who you are and what you did."

Esther thought she would feel jubilant, or at least gratified that her brother's killer would be brought to justice. Instead, she just felt sad. Grayson had taken her brother's life and had wasted his own life, as well as the lives of others.

About the time she heard the wail of police sirens sounding from the street, Esther heard pounding on her door. She opened the door and saw Stephen. Without a word she moved into his arms. He wrapped them around her in a strong, loving embrace. For that moment, all that mattered was that she was safe and she was with the man she loved.

The police chief and several officers crowded into her small living room.

"Esther, call your dog off of the suspect, please."

Maggie Jones' voice sounded tense.

Esther turned to see Ninja's teeth mere millimeters from Grayson's throat. She caught her breath. He was still snarling at the man who had killed his partner.

"Ninja, heel!" she called sharply.

The dog didn't move at first. Esther could almost feel the officers' guns pointed at the pair on the floor. Finally, Ninja turned and limped over to stand by Esther. He was still on alert with ominous growls rumbling from his chest.

Grayson got to his feet, his limbs shaking so hard he could barely stand. He attempted to smooth his rumpled hair and suit and put on an air of importance.

"I want that dog terminated and this woman arrested for owning a dangerous animal," he blustered. "That beast could have killed me!"

Maggie ignored his ranting.

"Richard Grayson, you are under arrest for the murder of Paul Daniels, the attempted murder of a K9 police officer, and the attempted murder of Esther Daniels."

As Grayson protested and struggled, a police officer clicked the handcuffs on him and led him outside, reading him his rights on the way.

Maggie turned to Esther and Stephen and gave them a triumphant grin.

"I love when it all comes together."

She looked closely at Esther.

"Are you okay? Did he hurt you? How did he wind up on the floor with Ninja on top of him anyway?"

Esther gave Maggie a rundown of the events from the time she came in the house and found Grayson inside. When she mentioned Grayson grabbing her and what she did, Stephen had to grin.

"Esther doesn't like to be grabbed," he chuckled.

As Maggie headed out the door, Stephen and Esther moved to walk with her to the car. Ninja was still growling low in his chest, his gaze zeroed in on the man he had just helped to capture.

"Esther, I think you had better leave Ninja inside. I don't want him to eat my prisoner." Maggie rubbed Ninja's head. He briefly wagged his tail, but still watched out the door.

Esther and Stephen followed Maggie outside, leaving Ninja to watch out the window. Suddenly a bullet whistled past them and embedded itself in a post on the porch. Stephen covered Esther, his shoulder screaming in pain.

Another bullet smashed into the back window of the police officer's car where the prisoner had just been secured. Grayson flinched as the bullet barely missed him, then ducked as much as he could below the window.

"Grayson!"

Ken Owens stepped out from behind the tree he had used for cover. Maggie and the other police officers drew their weapons. They carefully watched as the gunman held his ground. His weapon was lowered, but his grip showed he was ready to bring it up and shoot.

"Grayson, you murdered my son. By getting him involved in your filthy trade, you killed him as surely as putting the rope around his neck. Now I'm going to do everyone a favor and kill you."

"Mr. Owens, I'm Maggie Jones. I'm the police chief here. Please drop your weapon, sir. You are under arrest."

"I know who you are, ma'am, and I don't mean to disrespect you, but I will not drop my weapon. I am going to kill the man that ruined my son and caused his death. Then I will turn myself in."

"Wait!"

They were all startled to see Jesse run up. He had stood by quietly while Grayson was arrested. The two men had looked at each other for a long moment before Grayson was placed in the police officer's car. Now Jesse was standing in front of Ken Owens and in the way of Maggie and her officers.

"Jesse, get out of the way!"

Ken met Jesse's eyes.

"Son, you heard the police chief. I know you worked for Grayson. Did he ruin you too?"

Jesse gulped back a sob and nodded.

"He almost did, sir, but I came to my senses. But, Mr. Owens, if you kill Richard Grayson, he will ruin your life too."

"He already did."

"No, sir, not yet. I know he got Jimmy involved with selling drugs. I know your son killed himself in prison. But, Mr. Owens, God still has a plan for you. If you kill someone, if you kill this man, you will let him ruin your life. Is he really worth going to prison for?"

Ken Owens stared long and hard at Richard Grayson. The former businessman was sitting up again, glaring coldly at Owens and Jesse.

Jesse held out his hand, palm up.

"Please, Mr. Owens, don't let him ruin any more lives. Give me the gun and I'll give it to Police Chief Jones."

Ken regarded the younger man for a moment, then nodded once. He handed the gun to Jesse and raised his hands to signal his surrender to the police chief.

Maggie motioned to a police officer to take Ken Owens into custody. She walked up to Jesse and laid a hand on his shoulder.

"Jesse, that was very brave for you to do that."

Then she lightly knocked the side of his head.

"It was also incredibly stupid. You could have been killed."

Jesse let out a shaky breath.

"Yes, ma'am, you are right about both of those."

He looked like he was about to cry.

"I couldn't let Richard Grayson ruin anyone else's life like he was ruining mine."

"Come on, I want you to come with me to give a statement down at the station."

Maggie got in her car and signaled for Jesse to follow her. The other squad cars fell in line behind Jesse's truck.

The quiet was almost startling to Stephen and Esther.

"Esther, I'm sorry," Stephen began.

"Stephen, you were right," Esther spoke at the same time.

They laughed, then Stephen conceded, "Ladies first."

Now that he was here in front of her, Esther felt a little nervous. Was it too late?

"Stephen, you were right. God showed me I was living in fear instead of trusting Him with those I love."

She gazed at him, loving his serious deep brown eyes and the way his hair fell over his forehead.

"I don't want to live in fear anymore. I want to live in faith and love."

She wrapped her arms around his neck and pulled his head down for a kiss. Stephen complied willingly. When the kiss ended Esther snuggled next to him.

"Does this mean what I hope it means?"

Esther pulled back slightly so she could look into his face.

"It means I love you," she said simply.

Stephen whooped with joy and then kissed her soundly.

Chapter 27

Day after Thanksgiving

Stephen brushed his hands on his jeans and picked up the box of Christmas lights. He slid it onto a small table on the porch, then went to stand beside Esther, giving the yard an approving glance.

"I think we've just about got it covered outside, sweetheart. Your house and yard look very seasonal."

Esther finished giving the wreath a final touch, then turned to survey their work. The roof was lined with lights, the porch and its pillars had lit garland wrapped around them, and the small fir tree in the yard was decorated with strands of popcorn and berries.

"I love it!"

She hugged Stephen in delight and gave him a kiss on the cheek.

"You are a genius for arranging my wiring so I can turn it all on with one click."

Stephen held on to her and turned her face up to his for a soft kiss on her lips. She sighed and twined her arms around his neck, silently asking for a longer kiss. Stephen happily obliged, then stepped back.

"We better get inside before we get your neighbors talking about you," he laughed.

"Let 'em talk," she retorted with a happy grin.

Esther held the door for Stephen as he carried the box of lights and outside decorations into the house and set it on the coffee table. Ninja finished his curious sniffing of the yard and followed them into the house, trotting to his bed and plopping down with a grunt.

"Are you ready to decorate the tree now or do you need to take a break?"

Stephen smiled tenderly at the hopeful look he saw on Esther's face. He knew she loved getting her house decorated for the holidays. She had told him that she celebrated the season from the day after Thanksgiving through New Year's Day.

Stephen was feeling hopeful too, as well as extremely nervous.

"Sure, we can start on the tree. What do you want to do first?"

He started toward the closest box.

"Do you start with lights or garland?"

"Lights!" she promptly responded. "Once we get the lights on, everything else is easy." She stepped toward her stereo and turned on some Christmas music.

"We have to have the right atmosphere, you know."

"Absolutely," he agreed. "We can't decorate without 'Deck the Halls.'"

They strung the lights and garland, then turned to the ornaments.

"Esther, before we start on these, could we take a break for some coffee and cookies?"

Stephen needed her to leave the room for just a few minutes.

"Sure, but I can't believe you're hungry after the huge dinner you ate."

Esther hurried into the kitchen.

Stephen quietly stepped over to the box closest to the tree and looked inside. Perfect, he thought. The box was filled with shiny Christmas balls, their silver hooks gleaming in the lights from the tree. He gave a quick look toward the kitchen, then walked over to his coat and pulled out two items. Working quickly, he finished and laid something gently in the box of Christmas balls.

"Here you go, hot coffee and your favorite chocolate chip cookies."

Esther set the tray down on the coffee table and handed Stephen a steaming mug. She settled on the couch with her own drink and admired the tree.

"It already looks beautiful," she said dreamily.

Stephen just smiled and nodded, his heart thumping crazily. Esther looked over at him with concern.

"Are you okay?"

She laid her hand on his arm.

"I don't want to wear you out, you know. You *are* still recovering from a gunshot wound."

Stephen just smiled at her anxious tone.

"I'm fine, sweetheart."

He set down his mug and reached for her hand.

"Come on, let's get that tree decorated. I can't wait to see how it will look."

Esther jumped up eagerly and reached for the box of ornaments. Stephen intercepted her.

"How about if I hand them to you and you hang them where you want them?"

"That sounds good," she agreed.

Stephen handed her a few of the brightly colored balls which she hung at different levels on the tree. Then he handed her the one he had fixed. It was a clear round ball that could be opened and filled.

Esther took the ornament without looking at it at first, then did a double take.

"Stephen, where did this come from? It's not one of mine."

Then she noticed the small royal blue velvet box inside. Nestled in the box was a gold ring with a single sparkling diamond exquisitely set.

"Oh!"

Esther's eyes went wide as she gazed at the box and then at Stephen.

He took the ball from her trembling hands.

"Esther, you are an amazing woman."

His hands worked with the ornament as he shared his heart with her.

"You are beautiful, strong, intelligent, and one of the most loving and caring people I have ever known."

Stephen set aside the clear plastic ornament and knelt on one knee in front of Esther. Ninja got up and trotted over to see what was happening. He licked Stephen on the cheek and stood looking quizzically at him.

Stephen smiled.

"Of course, Ninja. You're part of this too. Esther, would you call Ninja to heel?"

Esther nodded and commanded Ninja. The big dog sat at her side. He seemed to know something was up. His ears were up and he watched with interest.

Stephen took her left hand and held up the open box.

"I love you, Esther Daniels, and I am asking you – will you marry me?"

Esther's eyes were full of unshed tears as she gazed into his face. She gave him a trembling and watery smile.

"Yes," she whispered. Then, louder, "Yes, I will marry you. Yes, yes, yes! I love you too!"

Stephen slid the ring onto her left hand, then stood and folded her into his arms. He pulled back and framed her face with his hands, gazing intently into her eyes.

"I love you so, so much," he whispered as he claimed her lips.

Ninja sat quietly for a minute, then woofed at the happy couple. They pulled back from each other to laugh at the K9.

"I think he approves," Esther declared.

She glanced at her mantel where her brother's pictured face seemed to smile at her.

"I think Paul would approve too. He told me that I needed someone like you in my life."

Stephen kissed her again.

"No," he whispered in her ear. "Not someone *like* me. You need *me* in your life."

Dear Reader,

Thank you for reading *Mistaken Target*. Even though Esther and Stephen experience quite a journey to find their happy ending, they do find it.

I'll admit, when I first thought of writing this book, Ninja was the central character. I love dogs and I love stories with dogs. However, this is a romantic suspense novel, so we need to have someone to have that romance.

Stephen is still hurting and blaming himself for his fiancée's murder. Esther is afraid to allow herself to love because she believes God will take away anyone she loves. They have a rocky start but soon become friends through a shared interest in old books. Although Esther wants nothing to do with dating or romance, that attraction keeps sparking between them.

Jesse starts off working for Grayson because he likes the extra money, but he quickly realizes he is working for a cold-blooded monster. Now he feels trapped. Later, Jesse begins to realize, with his Aunt Abigail's help, that he can break free from Grayson. We'll see more of Jesse in book 2 of the Forrestville series, *Hidden Target*. In fact, Jesse is one of the central characters in that book.

Writing my first book has now turned into the four-book Forrestville series. Several of the characters in *Mistaken Target* need their own story told.

My prayer for this book, and the books to follow, is that they will bless and encourage as well as entertain you.

Turn the page for a sneak peek at the prologue for *Hidden Target*.

All God's Blessings,
Tina Ann Middleton

HIDDEN TARGET

The Forrestville Series
Book Two

Tina Ann Middleton

Shield Of Faith

Publishing

Prologue

She had killed a man.

Rachel stared in a dazed horror at the limp body at her feet. She tried to check for a pulse in his neck, but her hands were shaking so hard she could barely turn the body over.

All she could think was that no one would believe it was self-defense. She was a domestic worker employed at the home of a wealthy man. The dead man was her employer's nephew, and probably his heir, since her employer had no children. Who would believe that she was trying to keep her victim from raping her?

Rachel shook herself as she realized that she needed to get out of there before someone came looking for her or for the man whose life she had just taken.

She began throwing her belongings into a battered suitcase. As she tossed her clothes and toiletries into the suitcase, she didn't notice the small velvet pouch peeking out of a side pocket. Packing didn't take long since she lived simply, with few earthly goods.

Rachel allowed herself a moment's gratitude that she had been paid that day and had cashed her check while running errands.

She forced herself to stop and take a few breaths so that she could remember what else she would need to take with her.

Groceries! Grabbing a plastic grocery bag, Rachel filled it with items that could be used for quick meals; things like peanut butter, crackers, fruit, cereal. She snatched up a small cooler and dumped all the ice from her small freezer into it. Then she settled her eggs, milk, and a few other small perishables in the ice.

Rachel snatched up a small saucepan and her cast iron skillet, as well as plastic plates and a few utensils.

She carried her bags out to her small sedan, then hurried back into the cottage to check for anything she might have missed. Tears ran down her cheeks as she gazed at the cozy space that had been her home since her parents died several years earlier. The body on the floor caused shudders to run through her small frame.

Why had this happened to her?

Made in the USA
Middletown, DE
16 November 2023

42886809R00123